PENGUIN BOOKS

If You Tell Me to Come,
I'll Drop Everything,
Just Tell Me to Come

...spinosa has won several battles with death, which is
... stories are so full of life.

...oert was born in Barcelona in 1973. At the age of thirteen,
...s diagnosed with cancer, an event that changed his life
...er. After ten years in and out of hospitals, when he was
... told that he had been cured of the disease, he realized
... illness had taught him that what is sad is not dying, but
... not knowing how to live.

...bert is now a beloved and bestselling author around the
... His books have sold more than two million copies and
...ranslated into more than forty languages.

If You Tell Me to Come, I'll Drop Everything, Just Tell Me to Come

ALBERT ESPINOSA

Translated by James Womack

PENGUIN BOOKS

PENGUIN BOOKS

UK | USA | Canada | Ireland | Australia
India | New Zealand | South Africa

Penguin Books is part of the Penguin Random House group of companies
whose addresses can be found at global.penguinrandomhouse.com.

First published in Spanish by Penguin Random House Grupo Editoria, S.A.U. 2011
This translation first published in Penguin Books 2017

001

Copyright © Albert Espinosa, 2011
Translation copyright © James Womack, 2017

The moral right of the author and the translator has been asserted

Set in 12.5/15.5 pt Garamond MT Std
Typeset by Jouve (UK), Milton Keynes
Printed in Great Britain by Clays Ltd, St Ives plc

A CIP catalogue record for this book is available from the British Library

ISBN: 978–1–846–14822–4

www.greenpenguin.co.uk

Dedicated to everyone who wants to keep on being different, to everyone who fights against those people who want us all to be the same.

Written during the summer of 2010 over land, sea and air, in Menorca, Ibiza, L'Escala, Cabrils, Barcelona, Las Pungolas, Zurich and Helsinki.

Just when you think you know all the answers, the Universe comes along and changes the questions.

Jorge Francisco Pinto, *maestro*

Contents

If You Tell Me to Come, I'll Drop Everything . . . Just Tell Me to Come

I remember it like it was yesterday. She said to me, 'Don't you want your whole life to be happy? To leave behind the things that hurt you? Don't you want to feel that you're in control of your life, and not just drifting along in its rip tide?'

And I didn't reply.

I just sighed, letting a load of air rush out through my nose. My broken tooth appeared in a hopeful smile.

I didn't say anything, because, when you spend years feeling like life is something that just happens to you, and not something that you make happen, then, sadly, you end up getting used to it being that way.

And then she said, 'You know that old song, the one that goes, "If you tell me to come, I'll drop everything"?'

I nodded, still saying nothing; the words wouldn't come out, emotion had too much of a grip on me. My throat caught, and no sound came.

She went on: 'Well, I always thought there was something missing from that line. It should be, "If you tell me to come, I'll drop everything . . . but tell me to come".'

And she looked at me. Then she asked me the questions

that I had been waiting for years for someone to ask: 'Do you want to take control of your life? Do you want every moment of it to be yours? Do you?'

And I said 'yes'. I said the loudest and most powerful 'yes' I had uttered in all my forty years on the planet.

A 'yes' that stood firmly against the resounding 'no' that I had heard only a few hours earlier.

And you'll need to understand this 'no' before I can talk any more about the 'yes'. If you don't, nothing will make any sense; you won't understand any of it.

So it's crucial that you know what happened in the hours before I met this woman, the woman who would change the way I saw my life, the way I saw my world.

So here goes, the 'no' . . .

2

It's Hard to Feel Good Saying 'I Love You' on Your Own

A few hours earlier I had argued with my girlfriend. There wasn't anything particularly unusual or serious about this; we'd been arguing a lot recently.

If anyone had seen us, they would probably have thought that we were about to break up, but that was just how we were on a daily basis.

It was half past seven in the morning. I guessed that it would be light outside soon, but we still needed another two hours or so to argue, and then at least twenty minutes of sex for things to calm down. Needing all this time gave me a strange sense of déjà vu.

Couples and their rituals. Couples and their codes.

Every couple has their unique code, their own way of arguing, of making love, of forgiving, of blaming one another.

But we broke our usual pattern that day; there was no two hours of arguing, no twenty minutes of sex afterwards. I knew it when I saw her looking at me. It was a look I didn't recognize, no words accompanied it.

Normally, whenever she looked at me, she spoke to me; this was one of the many things I liked about her. So, when she looked at me like that, without a sound, I froze, completely.

It was as if she was on the verge of saying something like, 'This isn't working', or 'I'm sick of arguing', or 'Why are we like this if we love each other so much?' But she just looked at me.

And it was in that exact moment, as she was looking at me – strange and intense – that I remembered a phrase I had heard a few months ago at a dance show.

It was a performance in memory of Freddie Mercury and other artists who had died young. Or maybe it was something else. I can't really remember.

I don't much like dancing myself, but I do love dance. I love to see bodies in motion, unfamiliar songs coming together with the rhythms of the choreography. It stimulates me – in the emotional sense, I mean.

And, from time to time, like on that night, I'll hear a phrase that hits me like an arrow, piercing straight into my heart.

That night, somewhere between one incredible movement and the next, the principal dancer cried out: 'You told us to make love, not war. And we listened to you. So why does love make war on us?'

I smiled as I remembered. And my girlfriend just kept on looking at me. Then she said: 'I have to leave you, Dani.'

I have to. I have to. That cut me.

I considered this for a moment. All of those verbs – 'have to', 'must' – always seemed elegant to me. There are few verbs that have such a precise meaning. You know that when you use them, you are taking a firm stance, coming down definitively on one side or the other of a question.

'You have to?' I asked.

'I have to.'

Another silence.

I had to try to convince her to stay.

And how better to do that than with our own special way of saying 'I love you'. Every couple has one. Our way came from the first film we saw together. It was a film that I had seen years before I met her, during a special time in my life, and because it meant so much to me, I had decided to share it with her.

It was Jean-Luc Godard's magnificent film *Breathless*. In it, the legendary actor Jean-Paul Belmondo is at his best – he was never more 'Belmondo' than in that movie.

Our special sequence takes place in a car; there's a lot of talking in the scene, but only three lines really stuck with us, and we would always say them to each other, one after the other, without stopping, just like we had first heard them, like they had struck us.

It was our way of saying 'I love you'. Whipping out those three little sentences had never before failed to calm down an argument or defuse some tense moment.

I was the one who would say the first and third lines; she would say the second. Although, actually, sometimes it was the other way round. It just depended on who needed to bring the other one back to sanity, back to love.

We barely ever used it.

The trick for something like this to work so magically is to use it only in desperate situations.

I looked straight at her; I wanted her to know that this was one of those moments.

'I can't live without you,' I said, putting as much Jean-Paul Belmondo into my face as possible.

She looked at me and said nothing. I tried again: 'I can't live without you.'

She kept looking at me.

Her eyes said 'no'. Then her head said 'no'. Then she said it out loud, the clearest 'no' I had ever heard in all my life. It was so absolute that I knew that everything was over.

Even though, maybe, it didn't have to be the end, her refusal to play our little game was a definite sign that it was all coming to an end.

I tried physical contact, my last resort. I moved towards her, but she waved me off before I could reach her.

I knew that there were at least fifteen good reasons why she might want to leave me, but there was one that seemed more likely than the rest.

And, just when I was about to ask her why she was leaving me, my work mobile began to ring. It only ever rang in extremely urgent cases.

I didn't know whether to pick it up, this was so clearly not the right time, and, if I did pick up, it would almost certainly be the straw that broke the camel's back. I don't know why I did, but I answered.

The moment I said 'hello', she got up and walked to our bedroom.

It was just then that I remembered some words of wisdom given to me by one of my gurus, a man I had met when I went to have my tonsils taken out, years ago.

I was only in the same hospital as him for a couple of days, back in my home town, but he left his mark on my life. It had been some time since I had thought about him, maybe too much time. But my girlfriend's 'no' had immediately brought him back into my mind.

I suppose that I should tell you about him, because if you don't know what I experienced at his side thirty years ago, it'll be difficult for you to understand why I am the way I am, and why she did not want to stay with me.

For better or for worse, I became who I am thanks to Mr Martin. It was his fault.

But, before my memory takes me further back into the past, with the strange soundtrack of her packing up her things in the other room, I need to say Godard's three sentences, the ones that once meant 'I love you'.

'I can't live without you.'

'Yes, you can.'

'Yes, but I don't want to.'

I whispered them to myself, softly.

But it's hard to feel good about saying 'I love you' on your own.

3

The Loneliness of Having
No One There, Waiting for You

The day I met Mr Martin, I had been sent to hospital, at the age of ten, to have my tonsils taken out. He was just about to say goodbye to a lung and a half.

I was so scared when I went into the room that I inadvertently managed to calm him down.

'I thought I was the most frightened person in the world, but you must be three times as scared as I am. That makes me feel much better,' he said, very seriously.

He was very big – over six and a half feet tall, and about twenty stone.

Everything about him was excessive, extreme: he was over ninety years old and his greyish beard foamed all over his face.

I would've been scared of him if I'd seen him in the street, but there, in a hospital gown that didn't even cover his backside, he seemed completely harmless.

My parents had already left me to go and fill in the hospital paperwork, and I felt relieved that he hadn't met them. Back then, I felt embarrassed by them.

My chief ally against this giant was a nurse who didn't seem to have much interest in me, but who was, at least, more or less normal in terms of height, weight and age.

But my human shield disappeared as soon as she had me settled into my vast hospital bed.

So I was left alone with the most immense, imposing person I'd ever shared a room with. No one had ever taken up so much of the oxygen in a room; I'd never been so aware of someone else's breathing.

We didn't say anything. He didn't take his eyes off me.

The first two minutes were extremely tense. He could smell my fear, but it didn't seem as if he was going to attack. Finally he broke the deadlock.

'My name is Martin. What's yours?'

He held out his hand. I didn't know whether to take it.

My parents had told me that I should never talk to strangers. Although in theory Mr Martin wasn't a complete stranger, because I'd be sleeping next to him for the next three nights, provided everything went smoothly.

It was odd. He was a stranger who would have to become, quickly, by force of circumstances, someone I knew very well.

'Dani.'

It was barely a whisper, but I think he heard me.

I took the hand he was holding out, and squeezed hard. He smiled, and didn't squeeze back. It was a nice gesture. He was letting me think I was stronger than him.

Just as I was about to say something else, a porter appeared to take him into surgery.

The man spoke to him with a distractingly loud voice.

It's odd how people think they need to talk like that to the elderly. As though they're somehow making things easier by shouting at them, or speaking extremely slowly.

'Hello, Mr Martin. It is time to go into surgery. Is there anyone waiting for you? Where is your companion?'

Mr Martin waved his hand to make him speak a little more quietly. The sight of it made me giggle . . .

'I don't have a companion,' he replied, without seeming to feel any kind of embarrassment.

'You don't have anyone to wait for you outside while they are operating?' the twenty-year-old orderly said, in a tone that was almost rude.

'Oh, I have lots of people who'll be there if things go wrong. There's just no one who'll be there if things go right.'

Now the porter was embarrassed.

'I'm sorry,' he murmured.

'I'm not. I'm not a part of this age any more. It's normal that my people wouldn't be here, isn't it?'

The three of us were silent.

I'd never imagined that there might be people who had no one to wait for them at the surgery door. No one that the doctors could talk to about what was happening, apologizing for the delays, explaining the complications and the problems.

'What are they going to do to you?' I asked, putting on my best adult voice.

He turned and looked over at me again.

'They're going to leave me with half a lung. Just enough

to breathe in and out a little. But I don't need much at my age. They've said that you can live with only a quarter of a lung. So I'll have more than enough.'

I was stunned. I was only there to get my tonsils taken out, and I had my mother, my two living grandparents and my brother with me. He was going to lose most of his lungs, and he had nobody there with him, waiting for him to come out of surgery.

I think this was the exact moment when I first realized that the world was unfair. Ever since that moment, I've seen so much injustice that I've stopped counting up the individual instances, living with them almost without being upset.

'I'll wait for you,' I said, almost without knowing what I was saying. 'I'll be your companion.'

He smiled for the first time. It was a very happy smile.

He came over to me and gave me a hug. And, as he hugged me, I felt his fear, all the fear that he had before that operation which would stop him from taking in as much air as he wanted, as much as he needed to breathe.

'Thank you,' he whispered. 'It's better for me to go in there knowing that someone will be waiting for me when I come out. It'll make me feel like I'm going through all this for someone, and that's important. Did you know that, in a theatre, they only put on the show if there are at least as many people in the audience as there are in the cast?'

I shook my head.

'Well, now I can act, because I have my audience. I'll do a good job for you.'

He let go of me and stopped whispering.

The porter took him away. Once I was on my own, I realized that I had taken on a great responsibility.

He would be in surgery for almost eight hours and I had decided to be a proper hospital companion to him.

A kid of ten responsible for a man of ninety.

It seemed perfectly normal to me at the time. Now, it seems a little odd.

Although everything seems a bit different now. Without her, without our code, our way of saying 'I love you', I feel a little bereft.

I know that you'll want to know whether Mr Martin came back from surgery with just half a lung left, but first I need to tell you more about my journey to meet that woman, the woman who thought that some love songs could do with having their titles extended.

So I need to go back to that phone call, to the new job I was being asked to take on.

4

Sometimes a Couple Has So Much Baggage That Not Even Love Can Lift Them Up

While she was getting all her stuff from our bedroom, I was in the living room talking on the phone. It was surreal.

I was overwhelmed, just by the noise of her putting her belongings into her suitcase. I knew that I'd take the case, whatever it was. I didn't want to stay alone in this room where we had just been arguing, far less in an empty apartment where she no longer lived.

I know I could have gone after her. She hadn't left yet, but we had had so many problems together, we were dragging so much of the past along with us that it was impossible for things to be solved like in a Hollywood movie.

It wouldn't have helped if I'd appeared at the door of the room, looked at her, moved her gently away from the suitcase, given her one of those incredible kisses and said that she shouldn't leave.

It wouldn't help, and I knew that. She needed someone who could tell her, promise her, things that I just couldn't at that moment.

Sometimes a couple has so much baggage that not even love can lift them up. Not even love.

I wrote on the piece of paper that I had taken to make notes on the phone call: 'Not even love.'

It's fascinating how the brain can give the hand an unconscious order and make it repeat whatever the heart is saying, words that have never been spoken aloud.

Thought can be so intense, it has the power to make even a simple idea take root in your mind, and then show you how firmly fixed it is.

I carried on taking down details of the job.

As always, the voice that was giving me the case was trying to sound calm, but I could sense an unbearable panic.

It was at least fifteen or sixteen times more panic-stricken than a child about to have his tonsils taken out. I always took that level of fear as the base level for my measurements.

'How old is the child?' I asked.

If the missing child was younger than eleven I never took the case. I was strict about that. I wish I had been as clear about other parts of my life.

'He's nearly ten,' the man on the telephone said. His voice trembled a little.

That already made it impossible for me to take the case, but I kept on talking. I suppose it was so as not to hang up and have to face her. I needed time to decide what to do, a little more time.

'How long ago did he disappear?'

If it was less than three days, or more than two years I didn't take the case either. It was another one of my rules.

24

With time, I have found that these codes make sense in the workplace, but never in your personal life.

'Two days. Exactly two days.'

Two out of two. This was not a case for me. I had to be realistic and make things clear to this man before he got his hopes up, and got it into his head that I could help him.

'Call the police,' I said, trying to sound as curt as possible. 'They'll be able to help you better than I can.'

Absolute silence.

I couldn't even hear him breathing. If your ten-year-old child has been missing for two days, your life breaks, you come close to the void. That's why you'll put all your hopes in anyone – or anything – that you think might bring them back to you.

I'm not being clever here; I know this for a fact. I have spent years looking for children and adolescents who have disappeared.

When I first started out, I didn't have any codes, and would take cases involving children younger than ten, but what I ended up finding hurt me.

I don't know exactly when it was that I decided on the rule – that I would only look for children over the age of ten. I think it was to keep myself from feeling unbearable pain. I rejected everything that caused me pain like that. Just as I did in almost every other aspect of my life.

I had always wanted to be a policeman, to investigate things. But most of all I wanted to look for people who had walked out on their lives without any explanation.

I suppose that I came to specialize in missing children

and adolescents because it's the only age group I really understand. I was happiest during my childhood. I think that's why it's easy for me to connect with people who aren't yet adults.

In theory, and in law, childhood and adolescence last up until the age of eighteen. I don't think that's true; lots of us live in perpetual adolescence, although for many of us it's almost unbearable.

I think that the best way for you to understand my obsession with loss, with children, with adolescents, with my work in general, would be to tell you about my own childhood and youth. Perhaps that's the best way for you to get to know me.

I heard the noise of the door closing.

She was gone.

The lonely silence of my apartment hit me all at once, and mixed with the silence of the man who was still waiting on the other end of the telephone.

Two different kinds of silence. They sounded different, but they had a lot in common. Shades of grey, shades of pain.

I went into our bedroom.

Her part of the wardrobe was completely empty. It was like being punched in the gut. I would never have imagined that empty drawers could still be so full with the essence of a person, or that that person could pack a life away so quickly into a suitcase.

The father on the other end of the line started to plead with me.

I couldn't tear my eyes away from those six drawers, all open to various degrees. They were like a staircase of despair.

I walked over to the bedside table.

I opened the two drawers that were always filled to bursting with all kinds of things. Maybe none of them was important, but as I'd always told her, anything that ended up in a bedside table had made it through the day, had gone with you to bed, and all the way to your dreams, into the night, so it must have some kind of value.

The first thing I looked at whenever I went into a child's room was the bedside table; that's where they would keep their most precious objects, the key to their little world.

But her things were no longer there.

There was nothing living in that little table. Both drawers were completely empty.

The father kept on offering me more and more money over the phone. I could not just be silent before this black hole of desperation.

'I'll take the case,' I said finally.

'Thank you, thank you,' he said, over and over.

I don't know how many times he thanked me. I knew I was breaking my own code, but I didn't care. The only thing I knew for sure was that I couldn't stay in that house any longer, not even for a night, surrounded by half-open empty drawers.

I was panicking. Out of control.

'Where do you live?'

I didn't just blurt out the question randomly. I didn't

want the disappearance to have taken place in my city, because I needed to leave, to get somewhere far away from my loss.

'Capri,' he answered. 'If it would help, I can send you all the information that I have about my son. They've given me an email address for you, I don't know if it's right, or else I could send it via fax, or . . .'

I didn't listen to him, even though I kept answering him. I gave him details about what he had to send me, and how, and where. About my rates and the kind of transport I needed. But I didn't pay any attention to what he said, as soon as I had found out that I would have to return to Capri. I had been there once before, when I was thirteen. The island had saved me.

And now I had to return to Capri, just when I was, once again, alone and lost. It was incredible; the island always rescued me just as the ground was falling away beneath my feet.

Capri was where I spent the final days of my childhood. Not because I grew older, but because, somehow, I grew up.

I'll need to tell you about Capri. And about George, the man who marked the end of my childhood.

5

Light Bulbs That Go on
When Others Go out

The first and only time I visited Capri, I was thirteen. I'd lost my tonsils three years earlier and, surprising though it may seem, I didn't miss them at all.

The biggest change of those three years was the appearance of a red mark on one side of my face, which would get darker whenever I blushed, embarrassed.

Sometimes I felt like a clown who was halfway through putting on his make-up, and I wasn't the only person to think so.

There were people at school who called me 'half-clown' and 'dwarf'. I could only be half a clown and not a real clown, they said, because I was missing the red patch on my other cheek. I'll tell you about the dwarf part later.

Because of this crappy nickname and because they often held me down and tried to draw the other patch on my cheek with a biro, I ended up spending almost every day fighting with the people who teased me. But I have never been strong, or tall, or a good fighter. So I'd always lose.

I'd often come home with a black eye above my red cheek. It was a hard thing for my parents to see. They'd try to cheer me up. But they were like me.

Looking back on it now, it's kind of funny. Obviously, then, it wasn't funny at all, but it really does seem funny now. Time has a knack of making you see the comedy in things that really, at the time, felt a lot more like tragedy.

The day that I ended up with a couple of cracked ribs and two black eyes was the day I decided to leave home.

I hated school. My parents could do nothing to help, even though they knew exactly what it was like. It was hard enough for them to deal with their own problems. I'll tell you about them later.

I remember that they were away that day, and I filled a little suitcase and decided to go off to a place where people weren't given black eyes all the time. I was sure that there had to be a place like that somewhere, though I wasn't entirely sure where.

But I didn't manage to get very far. I'd only just opened my front door, when I bumped into a policeman. I'd never thought that the police were so on the ball that they could stop children from running away from home before they'd even left. But he hadn't come to stop me from running away. He'd come to bring me news about my parents.

My parents died that day, the same day I tried to leave home. I will never get over it.

I was left in the care of my brother, who was eighteen years old by then, officially an adult. Nothing got better at school, and at home, everything got worse. My brother had always been a bastard, and when you are being parented by a bastard, things get pretty complicated pretty fast.

So, ten months after I lost my parents, I decided to run away again. This time there weren't any policemen waiting at the door.

And this time, I knew where I wanted to go. I wanted to go to a place that someone had once told me was pure magic. Magic in the form of an island. Capri.

But first I had to get to Naples. It took me several days to get there; it was an odyssey, but I'll spare you the details. And then I caught a ferry to Capri. And it was there, on that boat, that I met George.

George was sixty-three years old, and sturdily built. I longed to turn fourteen and get big and strong as quickly as possible. Between me and George were fifty years of experience, hope and longing.

We were both standing on the stern of the boat; we weren't particularly close to each other, but we weren't very far apart either. I wasn't taking any chances; I wasn't going to get close to anyone. All I wanted was to get to this magical, problem-free island.

I saw George watching me. I think he'd realized I was running away the moment he saw me get on the ferry.

No one, not since Mr Martin, has been able to judge my intentions so well without even exchanging a single word with me.

'Running away?' he said, in a voice just loud enough for me to hear, not taking his eyes off the pages of a yellow book that he was reading.

I panicked.

I had never thought that it would be so easy for someone to figure me out, to know exactly what was going on in my life.

I wanted to get far away from this man who had his eyes on his book, but was reading me. But something stopped me from going.

I didn't answer. He didn't repeat the question. But, after a few seconds, he spoke again: 'My name's George, and I'm going to Capri. What about you?'

It's been years, but even now, that rule of thumb, 'Don't speak to strangers', is so deeply ingrained that I find it difficult to carry on a conversation with anyone I don't know.

But I also knew that I needed to find someone, a companion, on this boat full of strangers. A thirteen-year-old boy travelling alone will always attract a lot of attention, and seeming to be with an adult would be the perfect disguise. I walked over towards him.

'I'm Dani, and I'm going to Capri too. Obviously. All of us are.'

He gave a dry laugh. It had a slow, even pitch. I liked it.

He held out his hand. I took it and squeezed hard. He didn't give in, and instead squeezed back even harder, so much so that I needed to let go in order for him to do the same. As far as the handshake went, he was completely different from Mr Martin.

I sat down next to him. It needed to look as if I was travelling with an adult; I needed to make it look like

I was his son or his nephew. Even so, I left a few inches between us.

I saw that he was reading a book of anecdotes about the lives of famous people. Strange and curious facts, the real-life stories behind the legends.

I read over his shoulder.

'Finding this interesting?' he said, not taking his eyes off the book.

'It does look interesting,' I replied.

He immediately shut the book and passed it to me. 'Here you go.'

'You're giving it to me? You've finished it?'

'No, but I think you'll get more out of it than I will. Plus, I've got to do my exercises,' he said, standing up.

'Exercises?'

'Yes. You know, exercise, sport. Do you play any sports?'

I didn't play any sports. My only form of exercise was trying to avoid getting beaten up.

Suddenly, as he stood up, I realized that this man had a false leg. It was almost unnoticeable, but the slight difference in height between the two was clear, if you looked for it. He realized I was looking at his legs, and looked at me, waiting for me to ask about the false one. But I didn't. I didn't want to pry.

'What kind of sport do you mean?' I asked, getting back on topic.

'Just exercise in general. Getting my body in shape. Arms, neck, legs. Well, leg in my case.'

No doubt he'd noticed me indiscreetly observing his leg. I didn't like the way he was hinting at it.

'And you're going to do your exercises on the boat?' I asked, refusing to play along.

'Is there any better place for exercise than this? The air is fresh, you're out at sea, and you have loads of time on your hands. Would you care to join me? If you take control of your body, maybe you'll decide not to run away.'

He knew more about me than I knew myself.

He held the book out to me again. I took it. He started to walk towards the prow of the boat; he limped very slightly.

I sat for a while before getting up. But eventually I followed him.

'The best one in there is the story about Edison, the guy who invented light bulbs,' he said, without turning round. 'Do you know who he is?'

I gave a sharp nod; I didn't want him to think I was ignorant.

'Before he died, he asked his son to take a test tube and use it to capture his dying breath.'

'Why?' I asked.

'Because Edison thought that last breath would contain his soul,' the man said, looking me in the eye.

He'd captured my attention.

'And his son did it?'

'Of course he did. This was the man who had invented the light bulb. If he said that's where his soul was, then that's where it had to be. His son waited patiently by the side of his father's bed until the old man gave out his last breath. And then he caught it.'

We were silent. I wanted him to go on.

'And his soul was there, in that last breath?' I asked, as though my own life depended on it.

'Maybe, maybe not. You should go to the museum in Michigan one day and have a look at the test tube yourself. I saw it once, and thought that the son had been wrong to use a test tube; he should have taken a light bulb, one with the end opened up, and caught the breath in there. I'm sure that then, as Edison's life went out, the bulb would have lit up.'

He stopped when we reached the prow, just next to the luggage area. He turned and looked straight at me. 'Are you ready to learn how to control your body?'

The sun was setting slowly above the boat as it headed towards Capri, and I felt I couldn't even begin to imagine all the things that this man might possibly teach me, this man who spoke of light bulbs and souls, who limped but who did sports, who knew that I was a runaway child, but who didn't seem to care in the least.

Everything is possible if you go to Capri. Maybe that's why I wanted to take this case.

I lost myself and found myself on that island. And now, years later, another child whose case didn't tick any of the right boxes was also lost out there.

I have a weakness for coincidences; a coincidence is the only thing in the world that can make me break my rules.

There was no doubt about it. I had to get to Capri.

'I can be in Naples in a couple of hours. Come and pick me up and we'll take the ferry to Capri together. All right?' I asked the lost boy's father over the phone.

He thanked me again before the call ended. Really, I was the grateful one; it was I who wanted to return to the island so badly.

I know I should carry on telling you about George, and the answer I gave him, but I need to head off to Naples first.

6

Forgetting a Scent Because You Are in a Hurry

I put a few things in a bag and booked myself onto the first flight to Naples. I knew that I was running away again. The fact that I'd just been dumped was starting to overwhelm me. So I tried not to think about it. It was a childish reaction, but just what I had to do in that moment.

I went to the bathroom to get a couple more things.

And it was there that I found her perfume. She had left it behind.

She had forgotten her scent because she was in a hurry. She'd only gone through the drawers and the bedside table.

I brought her scent up to my nose, and it was like having her by my side again. Just like feeling her next to me.

It hurt. I missed her already, and she had only walked out of my life ten minutes ago. This was going to be painful. That was for sure.

I think that now we've reached this point, I should tell you about the problems my girlfriend and I had. It's only fair, because if I don't, then you won't know whose side to take.

Let's not fool ourselves: in any break-up, you have to take sides. Always, even if you don't want to. Even if you're a part of the family, or a friend, or even just an innocent reader, you have to; you need to pick a side, if only to be at peace.

She and I – shit, it hurts to speak about this. I realized that I was covered in her scent. All I did was breathe it in once, and now I smelled like her.

I knew I should get rid of this giant bottle of perfume soon, before I ended up accidentally wearing her scent every morning. I had to pour it down the sink.

You have to understand that, with her smell on me, in the bathroom, the pain hit me even harder. I could barely take it.

So I decided to pour it down the toilet, and lifted the seat. But I paused. I couldn't just throw her scent away. It wasn't fair or right to do so. It almost made me feel sick. I stopped just before I'd begun to pour, before I lost a single drop.

And suddenly, I thought of a better way of getting rid of this perfume, without making myself feel guilty.

I stuffed the bottle into my bag.

I left the house in a hurry, without locking the door. I didn't care if anyone came in and took anything. There was nothing valuable left there.

I got a taxi straight away. It was one of those taxis that seemed to know just when you're leaving your house, a taxi that was turning the corner just as I shut my front door.

And there, in the taxi, in silence, I waited.

I just wanted to let the minutes go by until I reached the airport. I didn't need conversation, or music.

I just needed some time to pause, to get away from what was happening around me.

For many years I have needed to live in the moment. But now it was crucial that I did exactly the opposite, because that moment, that present moment, was not going to give me anything at all. It was the future, the future that had the key, the future that would give me back my own, healthy self.

I think that the last time I needed not to live in the moment was when I was waiting for Mr Martin to come out of the operating theatre. I just wanted the hours to go by and for him to come back, with the operation already finished. As I've said, I was his companion and I took my duties very seriously.

The taxi driver broke the silence and put on the radio.

A Colombian *vallenato* came on. It's always struck me as deeply sad music, too sad. Worst of all are the *boleros*: tales of lost love, impossible love, of love with no future. The singers luxuriating in their loss as though it were something beautiful. I can't stand *vallenato* songs.

This one was called 'I Had So Much Hope' and the lyrics chipped away at my soul minute by minute. I wanted to ask the taxi driver to turn the music off, but that would mean having to talk to him, which was precisely what I didn't want to do. I didn't want to interact with another human soul any more than strictly necessary.

So I decided to escape in my mind, away to that hospital where I waited as a child for a man to return with only one half of one lung remaining.

7

In This World, It Pays to Show Emotion You Don't Feel

Mr Martin went into surgery at eleven o'clock in the morning. A nurse came by at one in the afternoon to tell me that everything was going all right. I felt calm. Only six hours left.

My parents had gone off to eat somewhere, so I was alone in the room; Mr Martin's side of the room called to me, enticingly.

I wanted to know who this gigantic man really was, this man whom I was waiting for so eagerly. I think that it was my first ever investigation.

Though it wasn't the room of a missing child or a teenager that I was riffling through, the adrenaline that came pulsing into my veins as I went through this man's belongings was exactly the same as I would experience later. The feeling never changes; you always sense that same thrill in finding unfamiliar objects.

I felt I was within my rights to be looking through his things: I was waiting for this man, so at the very least, I thought, I ought to get to know him.

I opened the drawer of his bedside table. You already know what I think about those drawers.

There were letters, a little notebook and lots of Polaroid photos. It all looked as if it had come from another era.

I looked at the photos. They all showed lighthouses.

Lighthouses of all shapes and sizes. But none of the shots was taken from the land, and none of them showed Mr Martin.

They were all taken from boats, sometimes from far out at sea. In each photo, you got a glimpse of a prow or a stern or a mast, and then, in the background, an immense lighthouse. Most of the photos had been taken at night and showed the lighthouse in operation, its light moving.

There wasn't a single person visible in any of them.

Lighthouses and fragments of boats. Boats and fragments of lighthouses. There were almost five hundred of them: slowly, I counted each one as I looked at them. I had time enough to spare.

I saw that a date and a word were written on the back of every photo. The words were adjectives that didn't seem to bear any connection to the features of the lighthouse or the place or time when the photo had been taken. I was almost positive that they were about Mr Martin himself.

They were words like, 'sad', 'lovely', 'lonely', 'unfaithful', 'distant', 'alone'. One of them – 'lucky' – struck me deeply. It appeared on about a dozen photos. I remember realizing that this was the first time I had seen this word written down. In my world, people just weren't lucky, and it was even less likely to occur to them to write it down so as to have some memory of it for ever.

About four hours later, the nurse came back and told me

that they'd removed the lung and everything was fine. The nurse said, 'Your friend is a lucky man.'

I smiled. I knew it. I had been working this out as I looked through his belongings. I realized he was a fighter; he'd never give up. I could even see it in his handwriting.

My father always told me to practise neat handwriting, because that's how you show other people that you're trustworthy.

I think my handwriting shows that I'm trustworthy, so my father would be very proud of me. I don't know if he'd still be as proud if he knew that my job involved going through strangers' belongings. But he'll never know that.

I found lots of envelopes in Mr Martin's bedside table too. Inside each envelope was a list of numbers. Meaningless numbers: 12, 36, 9, 7, 2 . . . No rhyme or reason to them.

Each of the envelopes contained several sheets of paper, all covered in numbers. On the last page, there would always be two numbers written much larger than the others. And on the outside of each envelope was the name of a city.

It looked like the key to something, but I couldn't work out what. Perhaps Mr Martin was a spy. I looked at those two final numbers on the final page of one of the letters, written in red ink and trustworthy handwriting.

I found myself becoming fascinated by this mysterious man, and I didn't want to let him go without having got to know him better.

Realizing I felt this way towards him gave me goosebumps.

Though for me, there's nothing unusual about that, and

I'll tell you why. I can give myself goosebumps at will. My mother could do it as well.

When I was little, whenever I told my mother something important, or brought her back some work I'd done in school, she would always say to me that I'd given her goosebumps.

I believed it, and I felt glad that my mother was so sensitive, that she cared so much.

Until one day, my older brother told me that this was a trick we could all pull off – we all had the odd ability to give ourselves goosebumps at will.

I didn't believe him; I almost felt that he was insulting me. I remember trying to hit him and, although we were basically the same height and build, I ended up face down on the floor with him punching me, again and again.

I think the time has now come for me to tell you something that I haven't yet mentioned, but which is, I think, essential for you to be able to understand me, my family, and why I kept on running away.

I guess I should have mentioned this first of all.

My brother was a dwarf. Like my parents. And like me.

Yep, a dwarf. A 'little person', as the politically correct people have it. Yes, one of them.

When you're ten years old, the difference between a little person and a little boy is insignificant; you can't really see it at all, although I suspect that Mr Martin guessed as soon as he saw me.

When I was thirteen, though, the difference started to become clear, at least clear enough for me to end up the laughing stock of my school. Everything changed. My life slowly became unbearable, especially at break-times. I was 'half-clown' because of my red cheeks and 'dwarf' because, yes, I really was a dwarf.

But I was thirteen and I still expected to grow a little. I wanted to grow. The boys my age were only a couple of inches taller than me. Maybe I was only a bit short for my age, but I'd surely have my growth spurt one of these days.

I remember promising my mother that one day I would grow. As always, she got all emotional and said I'd given her goosebumps. Still, today, I hope that she wasn't just faking it. I need to believe it was true. My mother's emotions, her passionate belief in me, were what spurred me on, for years: I had to grow, had to grow for her.

She taught me that there was nothing sad or shameful about being a dwarf, but she also always dreamed that one day I would grow. The two things weren't incompatible. She told me that from the first moment she felt me inside her womb she had thought that I weighed too much, that I was a little giant. She told me this with affection, with pride.

She always said that a mother who was a dwarf could want to give birth to a giant without feeling embarrassed about what her fellow dwarves might think. Just as a gigantic mother might want to have a tiny baby for her own reasons.

I liked that she called other women gigantic.

When we were alone, she always called me her 'little giant'. It was a pet name that deeply annoyed my brother.

And so there I was, my face against the floor, pinned down by my brother's little hands. This was when he showed me that he, too, could give himself goosebumps if he wanted; he did so in front of me.

'You see how excited I get when I'm hitting you, little giant?' he said, as he banged my head against the tiled floor.

Then he started laughing.

I was half-angry, half-sad. My mother had been having me on for years.

I decided to see if I could do it, if I had the gift too.

In just a few seconds I saw all the hairs on my arm stand up and the skin pucker. It was incredible; I had this minor superpower, too. I didn't know what use it would be to me in the future, but I was sure that in the long run I'd find something to do with it.

Because, in this world, it pays to show emotion you don't feel. Although I didn't give any of that much thought at the time.

When my brother let me go I went straight to my mother.

Back then, my mother and I were dwarves of the same height. So when we spoke, we were level, face to face. There's something that's very odd about this between a mother and a son. I don't know why, but your mother should be taller than you while you're young, in order for you to feel safe, protected.

I told her everything, let everything out.

I felt cheated by her fake show of emotion. She didn't

say anything as I went on, but when I stopped shouting she burst into tears.

It was the first time I had ever seen her cry, and it was my fault.

For a moment, I wondered if her tears were real, or if crying on cue was another superpower I didn't know about. But I immediately realized that her emotion had hit me so hard, it was impossible to believe it was false.

'Dani,' she said between sobs, 'the fact that I'm able to do this doesn't mean that I have ever done it to you. Never. I've never done it. Everything you do makes me emotional, just because it's a part of who you are. You are the most important thing in my life, my little giant.'

I almost didn't hear her. Her words had the opposite effect from what she intended. I stopped believing that I would grow. I decided to run away from home for the first time.

Then, two days after this conversation, I lost her. Two days after I made her cry, she and my father died in the car accident. That damn accident. I can still remember the policeman trying to show pain and compassion in his voice, even though it was clear that he was only playing a role. A good old chunk of theatre to console one more orphan.

Ever since that day I've hated cars, hated people who drink and drive. I hate people who don't respect the speed limit, who say that they've got it all under control. They can't control anything. And then they send another family spinning off into the void.

I've had several altercations, almost fights, with people

who don't obey speed limits. They think they're the best, but they're nothing but arseholes.

The fact that someone thought they were above the rules is the reason my parents were killed. I can't allow anyone else to do that.

The funeral was the hardest part. Two small coffins.

I remember that the people in the next room along at the funeral parlour thought that two children were being buried. They gossiped about how terrible it must be for a parent to lose two children. That really stung.

I went over to one of the gossips and said, 'Those children are my parents. No one will ever be able to measure up to them.'

I know that I was out of control when I said that. But it still hurts, even after so many years. I think it'll always be an open wound. One that no one will ever be able to cure, ever.

But let's go back to the hospital; that's the story I want to tell you now.

Let's get back to the room that I never shared with Mr Martin.

I think I was telling you how I was going through his personal belongings.

The last thing I found in the bedside table was a little round object with glass set in the middle. It looked like a monocle, but the glass was tinted black and it had a handle in the shape of a lighthouse on the side. A silver lighthouse stuck to a kind of monocle; it was strange, but the two objects were so lovingly fixed together that they gave the impression of never having been apart.

It was an object that seemed to have a magic power.

I put it over my left eye, hoping to feel something extraordinary. But I didn't notice any change, except that the room got a little darker. It was just then, just during this eclipse, that the nurse came in.

She looked sad. I sensed that she came with bad news. Or maybe it was just the effect of the darkness that came from looking through the strange object.

'Dani, there's been a complication. Mr Martin is in the intensive care unit. He wants to see you.'

I didn't react. I didn't even take the strange glass away from my eye. I couldn't. All around me was black. It was as if the world had come to a standstill. I didn't want to go back to the normal world, back to being a companion.

I'd felt it was all a kind of game, a game I'd made up, a game where a ten-year-old boy looks after a ninety-year-old man. I had never thought that I'd have to hold a wake for him.

'That's twenty-nine euros thirty-five,' the taxi driver said, breaking me out of my sad childhood memory.

Don't worry; I'll be back there again, soon enough.

The best thing about memory is that it lets you travel whenever you want, and no one can stop you.

What's odd about it, though, the most striking thing, is that whenever you return, the memory changes.

And as the memory changes, you change too. Because that's where your roots are, and if the roots change, then the whole plant above it has to change as well.

'Love' Is a Verb That Only Has a Past Tense

I've never liked airports. I've always thought that there are too many barriers to get through before you can enjoy the peace of being on the plane.

Border controls, check-in, the fear of losing your luggage: these places are terrible.

I once read a study that said that a person's heart rate increases palpably as soon as they enter an airport.

And this increase is due to so many things: the rush to find a check-in point; the rush to then check everything in, or, to try to check in nothing at all, or the fear that you'll still be made to check everything in; the rush to find the perfect seat; the rush through security; the rush to be first in the boarding queue, so that you can store your luggage in the overhead locker and it doesn't need to be sent to the hold; the jittery take-off; the fear whenever there's a moment of turbulence; the fear that comes with the landing; the urgent desire to get off the plane as soon as possible, to find the baggage carousel, get out of the airport and finally to reach your actual destination.

The most incredible thing the study reveals is that the thing which alters the heart rate least of all is the journey itself, and what quickens it most is the search for somewhere to put our carry-on luggage. How important it is to us to have our belongings close by. And the ideal, of course, being to have them stored directly over our heads.

Human beings are strange and complex.

So there I was, standing at the security checkpoint, my heart rate mildly elevated.

I think I'd never been so agitated before in my life. I wanted them to stop me as soon as they saw the suitcase on the X-ray, to tell me that rules were rules, to announce that travelling with such a large bottle of perfume was prohibited.

Like I said, I could have just got rid of her scent, but, if I put it in the suitcase and someone else confiscated it, then they'd be the one charged with the task of destroying it or getting rid of it by some other means, and this, according to my new post-break-up code, was A-OK.

I know that this was just as cowardly, but at least then I wouldn't have to be the one who was casting her away, by getting rid of her smell.

Before I put my suitcase on the conveyor belt, I thought that, for once, this stupid rule about transporting liquids would make some kind of sense, that it would give someone with a ruined heart the chance to start to heal.

I left the suitcase with her scent inside it on the conveyor belt, and little by little it was dragged along into the X-ray chamber.

I felt that when the security guard looked at his screen he would see not only a bottle of perfume, but also my entire life, my break-up and all of my problems with her.

She and I had a lot of problems. I know, I haven't forgotten – I need to tell you about my problems living as one half of a couple.

I just don't really know where to start. I'm the bad guy here. Don't expect me to say: 'I did this, and this, but then she did this, and she did that.'

She . . . She loved me. She did. She always loved me.

Mr Martin once said to me in the hospital that to love was simply to desire something a great deal. 'If you desire something, then you love it, it's the next stage, it's automatic, you don't need to look any further.'

But then George, my unlikely companion on the boat to Capri, had said that loving was remembering that you had desired and had been desired – but only ever in the past.

For George, 'love' is a verb that only has a past tense. I loved. Desire in the present tense, love in the past.

George. Mr Martin. I learnt so much from them, without trying. It all floods back to me now.

The suitcase was taking so long to pass through the X-ray that my mind drifted back to that stocky man who had helped me, back when I was a lost boy running away from home.

The truth is, when I found myself on that boat to Capri, I felt just like that suitcase, trying to get through security.

I was trying to fool him, to make him think that I wasn't a child who had run away, but a young man travelling on his own, but he knew this wasn't true.

61

He must have had some kind of X-ray machine inside him that meant he could see right through me. See what I had hidden and what my secret thoughts, hopes and fears were. He recognized my scent. He could smell my fear, the fact that I was completely lost, but he never called me out on it; he let me pass through because he knew I needed to make this journey, to make it alongside him.

I remember George saying, just as we reached his exercise spot on the boat, saying something that I've never forgotten, that I will never forget: 'It's better to lose yourself if you're young. Because if you lose yourself when you're young . . .

9

If You Lose Yourself When You're Young, Then You Won't Lose Yourself When You're Older

'. . . then you won't lose yourself when you're older.' Then he winked.

How could George tell that I was so lost?

I didn't say anything. Nothing at all.

He looked at me and asked how old I was. I realized then that he must know something about me, about my world, my life as a dwarf. That he must expect my reply to reveal my lies, my escape and my fear.

I lied and told him that I was nearly fifteen. I know he didn't believe me. But I didn't want to own up to only being thirteen, or the fact that I was a dwarf, or that I felt all alone in the world. I didn't want to tell him anything about my parents' death, or that I was in the care of a brother who hated me.

As the months had gone by, my brother had become even angrier, more volatile. Though I wasn't exactly cheerful myself. My father's death, my mother's death. Both hurt. Both were unbearable.

We fought every day. Every time I saw him, every time I remembered the promise I had made my mother, I hated being a dwarf, I was disgusted by how small I was, by my strange reflection in the mirror.

The truth is that, back then, I still looked like a boy, and not a dwarf. When you're thirteen, some kids are short because they haven't had their growth spurt yet, but by fourteen everyone has had it. Although, saying that, at thirteen there are already some real giraffes around, kids who have got tall and will only carry on getting taller.

I knew that if I hadn't had my growth spurt by the end of the year, then I would be officially small for my age. Officially, I would be a dwarf.

The doctors said that anything was possible. My genetic make-up was a mystery to them, and it was possible, they said, that I could be a dwarf or, as my mother said, that I could be a giant.

The absolute cut-off point, for them, was the age of fourteen. There was no way back after fourteen, they would then be able to see if my growth had actually stopped. Perhaps that was why I told George that I was fifteen. So that I could place myself beyond the uncertainty, at an age where everything had already been and gone.

I lied to him about my reasons for running away from home simply because the real reasons were too painful to speak about.

Part of it was because of the bullying that I'd suffered at school, part of it was because of my parents' death, and part of it, the last big part, was because I was a dwarf, and because I'd been left in the care of a brother with whom I felt no connection at all. I'll explain why if I ever feel I'm brave enough.

To be a dwarf for the rest of my life – I must confess that the idea scared me.

I wanted, no, I desperately longed, to be tall and strong. To grow.

It's difficult to put it into words, but knowing that you'll never grow, that your pencil mark on the door jamb will never go any higher, is terrible for a child, and unbearable for an adult.

And it has nothing to do with what it means to be a dwarf. My parents had always been proud of who and what they were, they were never ashamed.

And I'd dealt with it well enough, in my way. Ever since I was five I'd been more or less conscious that we were a different kind of family. We were like other families, but we were shorter. My brother was short, my parents as well; and I was the shortest of all. Well, at least until we bought a little dog, a dachshund. Everything just right, arranged to fit with our height.

But after my parents died, I needed to change, to leave behind what they had been, what we had been together, and turn myself into something completely different.

I think that it was my way of stepping away from my pain. Growing would make everything more bearable, because I would get away from them and it would, somehow, be easier to forget their death, their burial, the pain it caused me to have lost them for ever.

George went off to find something in the baggage area. It was as if he were inhabiting a completely separate universe, far away from all the thoughts that his question about my age had stirred up in me. Or else he realized he had stirred them up, and was giving me a few seconds to let them settle down again.

A few minutes later, he came back with a heavy red punch bag, and hung it from a hook on one of the posts on the ferry that had seemed to be of no use at all, right up until the moment that he found a perfect use for it. Or maybe its fate had been to wait for this moment.

I thought it was odd that he was carrying this huge bag on the boat. I couldn't even imagine how much it weighed, but it looked to me like it must have been a tonne at least.

'Did you bring the punch bag as your luggage?' I asked finally.

'It's not a punch bag; it's a part of my life. It's like my son; it goes with me everywhere I go.'

'Your punch bag is like your son?' I laughed. I hadn't laughed for days.

Forgetting to laugh is unforgivable, at any age. A mortal sin for a child.

'You don't like people laughing at you, right?' he said seriously. 'Right?'

'No, I don't like it,' I admitted. 'People laugh at me all the time, and do loads of other things as well.'

'Well, I don't like it either,' he said brusquely. 'This bag is my most important possession. And it takes punches like nothing else. Any time you hit it, whether you're angry, or if you've got a problem to fix, or if something horrible has happened to you, then the bag takes the blow, understands it, and makes you feel better.'

A gentle breeze passed over our faces. It smelt of the sea, reminding me of where I was.

I couldn't stop looking at the magic bag. George did not stop looking at me.

'Does it really take away your problems?' I asked.

'It does. Do you have a lot of problems?'

'A few,' I said, very seriously.

He did not laugh. I felt grateful. He looked straight at me and asked the same question again.

'How old are you?'

He hadn't believed my lie. And I still didn't want to answer the question, because of all that it might suggest, but I felt I needed to confide in somebody.

'Thirteen.'

'You must be very brave to leave home at thirteen.' He looked at me with respect and then continued. 'If a child leaves home at that age, it's because he feels he has to do so in order to survive. In order to grow. Is that your problem?'

I nodded. I didn't want to go into any detail. But I felt a lump in my throat when I heard him say 'grow'. I know that he was talking in a figurative sense, but he had hit the nail on the head.

'Hit the bag,' he said. 'You'll feel better. Much better.'

I was just about to hit the bag, hit it angrily, but before I did, I paused and looked at him. I asked him the question that I had wanted to ask for a while now, and which was worrying me quite a bit.

'Aren't you scared of being seen with a child?'

'Scared of being seen with a child?' he repeated. 'Are you going to hit the bag so hard that I'll be afraid to stand near you?'

He smiled. So did I. That was funny.

'You know what I mean. The people on the boat must have realized that I'm on my own. And I'm short, so I might even look like I'm eight or nine years old. And you've taken me over here, to the other side of the boat away from everyone, and you're spending your whole time talking to me,' I insisted, trying to make myself clearer.

'You aren't a child to me, you are a force of nature, pure energy,' he replied. 'An unstable energy.'

When he said these words, George made me think again of Mr Martin.

I know that Mr Martin had been about to die, and that he was weak in his hospital bed, and that George was in his prime and on a boat heading out to Capri. But both of them had a kind of strength about them, a strength that helped me find a sort of balance. As though they had come into, become a part of, my world. And when they spoke, I was totally arrested, absorbed by what they had to say to me. I've found very few people who have been able to do that in this world, though I've never stopped looking for them.

And though I wasn't aware of it, at that moment, on that boat, I was about to be given the most important lesson of my life.

Well – maybe the old woman who spoke to me about the song 'If You Tell Me to Come . . .' will turn out to have given me a more important lesson. It's hard to tell. You can't really number these things in a list like that. Especially because the way you take them in can completely change, from one year to the next. The way you understand things when you're thirteen is different to the way you do once you're fourteen.

But let's get back to that moment, when George shared his theory with me, when he imparted his lesson.

As always in life, I didn't pay all that much attention to it at the time. It's only now that I understand it entirely. I don't know how I could have spent so many years turning my back on his words.

'We are all made of energy,' he said as he lifted up the bag, standing still, waiting for me to punch. 'And energy is the only thing I see in this world. Each of us has a different kind of energy. Each person has a kind of energy that floods into you when you see them, or hear them, or desire them, or tell them you love them. And their energy can allow you to find your path through the world. You can't fake energy, it is what it is. It can help you find your future, it can take you back to your childhood or adolescence. I'm always looking for energy. I don't care about a person's age, or sex, or the way they look. Underneath it all, behind every body, behind every word, behind love, behind desire, you find these powerful energies. We all have to hunt for these energies, Dani. And if you do some exercise, get in shape, then you'll be a better hunter. Work on improving your body and your own energies, and then you'll be focused, capable of finding the other energies that you

71

need, in other people. Do you know how many kinds of energy you need to find for your life to be complete?'

I barely understood what he was saying, but I answered him, shaking my head. I didn't want him to stop.

'Just four. You just need four energies to have an impact on you. That's enough.' He looked me in the eye. 'Hit the bag. Go on. Hit it with all your anger. Turn your problem into a blow, a punch, and hit the bag. It'll do you good, I promise.'

I thought about my arsehole brother, about how badly he was treating me. I hope I can brace myself and tell you about him at some point.

I thought about my parents' death. About how much I still needed them. And about how happy they would have been to see me grow. And about how powerless I felt, because I wasn't growing, and the new powerlessness I felt as I headed into the unknown, how afraid I was.

I swung my fist with all the force in my arm and all the intensity of my problems and all the power of my worries.

At the last moment I added loneliness, grief and the lack of love to the list.

It all came together to make the impact of the punch, when it finally hit the bag, impressive. I was sure that this was the first time that the bag could have been given a blow made up of so many fragments of so many different problems.

I thought that I might be about to break a few fingers, but instead I felt the bag accepting the blow and saw my bony little hand sinking deep into the fabric.

I felt a strange pleasure.

My pain had turned into pleasure. I smiled.

'Do you have anywhere to stay?' George said, looking out from the boat. We were coming into port.

I shook my head.

'Would you like to come home?' he asked.

I liked that he said 'come home' and not 'come to my home'. As though it were both of ours.

I nodded. I wasn't afraid of him.

I turned and punched the bag four more times, and then another four. And so on, until I reached a round twenty. And then twenty more, and then another forty.

I think I must have hit the bag about two hundred times, and little by little I started to feel better, even though I was shaking more and more as I kept on punching. I felt the bag taking in all my anger and giving me pleasure and happiness in return.

My anger had been taken in, taken away.

If only I still had that bag. There was so much anger, so many problems, that I needed it to take away.

10

Red Handkerchiefs
Cover Up Bruises

If only I still had it. The man at the checkpoint called to me.

I smiled, relieved. I think I must be the first person ever to be relieved to be called over by security at an airport.

'Is this your bag?'

'Yep,' I said, hopeful.

'You've got a prohibited item in here,' he said.

'I do?' I said, trying to act surprised.

I don't know why I did, but at that moment I just felt like doing a bit of acting.

He started to open my bag. I smiled with relief; I was desperate to get rid of her perfume.

'What are you so happy about?' the man in uniform asked me, a little suspiciously.

'Nothing,' I replied. 'Just a private joke.'

He plunged his hands into my bag, and started carelessly rummaging through my things.

I breathed calmly. If he confiscated it, I'd be able to take control of myself again. I needed to regain my balance.

But maybe this would all be too hard. To lose her smell would be like losing her for a second time.

Instinctively, while he went through my bag, I looked at my phone. I hoped I'd find a message from her, something that would make me think I could still save our relationship.

But there was no sign of her on the screen.

It was like being punched in the gut. The worst thing about break-ups is that if, immediately afterwards, there's no sign of regret, everything is definitely over. If there is any remorse, any regret, then maybe there's a chance that things can still be resolved.

'You can't take this with you.' He took my silver lighthouse with the monocle out of my suitcase. It was my most treasured possession.

I waited for him to take something else out. But he shut the suitcase again straight away. It was impossible – surely, he must have seen the bottle of perfume.

Incredible how red handkerchiefs can cover up bruises.

The man held my metal lighthouse in his hands and gave me such an angry look that it was as if he had just found a pearl-handled revolver.

'That's just a lighthouse with a monocle on the end, it's not dangerous at all,' I explained. 'It couldn't be used to kill or hurt anyone.'

'If you take the monocle off, it could be sharp,' he said, touching one end of the lighthouse.

'And if I filled it with bullets it could be turned into a machine gun,' I said, getting impatient.

He looked at me, sullen. I think he'd missed my irony. The worst thing you can do with these people is laugh at them. Because that's how you bring out their mean side.

'I'm going to have to confiscate it,' he said, in a voice that both showed off his authority, and showed me how much I'd pissed him off.

When I heard this, when I thought that I might lose the lighthouse for ever, my wild side sprang into action. The dark side that we all have inside us. When I get angry, I lose control; it's like a switch is flicked, and something inside me gets turned on that won't switch off until I've let everything out.

It's injustice that sets it off – the pain of others, my own pain, humiliation and incomprehension.

And when it's set off, my eyes get so fierce, so intense, it looks like I'm capable of doing something really crazy. My voice gets louder, and I'm not able to calm down until I've let everything out.

I almost never manage to get what I want when I'm in this state, but at least I let off some steam.

I know that I could work on changing this, but I also know that it's a part of my nature, that it balances me out.

And so I started to lose control. I started to shout at this man, to try to make him understand that this lighthouse was a gift, one which I could not allow myself to lose, not ever. I told him that I always carried it with me, that it made me feel safe, that I could not, would not, abandon it for anything. I said all this in the most aggressive, insulting way I could think of, swearing the whole way through.

I have to confess that it wasn't really me saying those words: they were the words of a ten-year-old kid, one who was waiting for an old man to make it through an operation, who had been given lots of emotional support and a little object in the shape of a lighthouse by the old man. The lighthouse was his parting gift. I promised him that I'd never lose it, that I'd always take great care of it.

Those last hours with Mr Martin are a part of who I am, they're a part of my DNA. A part of my life back then as a dwarf, a young dwarf that someone, for once, decided to treat like an adult.

I've always thought that, in life, there are people who nourish you, who love you, people you need so much that you can never fill the hole they leave behind when they're gone.

Losing my parents so young meant I never got the chance to have those silly little phone calls, them just calling to hear my voice, to ask me how I'm doing, how things are going, to hear all the little details of my daily routine.

Whenever my girlfriend's mother called to ask her how she was, how things were going, and had she taken her coat down from the loft because winter was on its way, I would always feel so jealous.

I wish I'd had a person like that in my life. A mother or a father who would ring me to ask if I was going to eat with them that Sunday, or if I was all right, if I was happy, if I had enough socks, if I was saving any money, if I was sure that she was the right one for me, if I was going to have kids, where I was going to send them to school.

My parents left, and no one ever asked me these questions. My brother could have taken on that role, but he hasn't spoken to me for almost a decade.

The fact that I ended up a few centimetres taller than him has come between us. Although it wasn't just a question of height. It was, ultimately, a matter of whether or not we were proud of our parents.

He could never understood that my wanting to grow had nothing to do with pride, that it was instead to do with keeping a promise I'd made, even if the people to whom I had made that promise were no longer with us.

Losing Mr Martin meant I lost other things, too. Because, when he passed away, a part of my childhood ended: my childish belief that death was something that happened to other people, that it had nothing at all to do with me. How wrong I was.

I was still shouting at the security guard when my phone started to ring. It was the man from Capri; he was getting nervous, his son needed me. And here I was thinking about Mr Martin and getting my lighthouse back.

A lost child and a lighthouse about to be lost.

They Are a Part of Me, Reflections of What I See

I stepped slowly into the ICU, and felt everyone turning to look at me.

I was scared. I knew I was Mr Martin's companion, and that I had to be with him, but all of this made me feel panicky. I'd only gone into the hospital to have my tonsils taken out. My time there should have, in theory, been very short. The ICU was not on my itinerary.

The patients kept on staring. Although the difference at that time between a dwarf and a child was very slight, I think they sensed something different in me.

The nurse who had come to get me from the room walked ahead, and I followed her in the way people do when they are being taken into the presence of a person who has asked for them to come urgently.

At one point, I decided to look down at my feet; I couldn't bear to see the residents of the ward any longer, where the sounds of screams and snores and stifled pain all mixed together.

The variety and range of these different sounds gave me goosebumps. I had not yet discovered my superpower. It was the real deal.

We got to the far end of the room, and I saw him.

He looked about five years older, although it had only been five hours.

Sitting there with his torso exposed and covered in gauze, he almost had the air of a maharajah.

There were dozens of tubes coming out of his body, carrying bits of him away from himself.

'I'll come back in a bit, you just sit here next to him for now,' the nurse said, pulling up a little wooden stool.

I took the stool in one hand and walked with it to the side of the bed. In my other hand I was clutching the things I had found in his bedside table. A few photographs of the lighthouses; the list of numbers; the strange object, half lighthouse and half monocle.

His breathing was loud and heavy. It sounded like he was doing enough breathing for four people.

His eyes were gently shut, I imagined because of the anaesthetic.

It was the same Mr Martin that I'd met a few hours ago, but now he seemed lethargic, weak. He was like a wounded animal, a creature mercilessly shot down.

It took me a while to sit down by his side. I stood there with the wooden stool in one hand, and his belongings in the other, feeling the strange thrill of holding things you've stolen from someone else.

I felt like an intruder, there in the ICU; that's why I was scared to sit next to him.

I felt like I was taking the place of someone who knew him better, someone who understood his world, someone more worthy of being next to him in this moment.

But there was no one else there. And he'd already said that he didn't have anyone like that in the world.

I paused again, but eventually decided to sit down at his side.

I put the chair down carefully, next to the drip they were using to feed him. I judged that the best place for me to be was there, under the contraption that was keeping him alive.

I put the letters, the photos and the strange object on a small table by his side. It was odd to think that these things had simply moved from one bedside table to another.

Mr Martin's eyes were still shut. His left hand lay close to mine, fingers gently spread.

I put my hand closer to his, but didn't touch it; I kept about half a centimetre away.

I felt I didn't know him well enough to take his hand, even though he was close to death.

That thought flickered in my mind for just a moment, but it must have been a very intense thought, a very intense moment, because, suddenly, I heard him speak.

'Are you afraid of taking a dying man's hand, Dani?'

I felt scared.

I looked at him. His eyes opened slightly. He was looking at me.

His gaze had the same intensity as it did when I first met him, but it was as if the life-fuel that flowed through his veins was a little less potent. Something in him was moving at a different speed, a slower rhythm.

You could see his strength, but also that soon he would seize up and stop moving.

I smiled and took his hand. It was instinctive.

'I think I've still got a lung,' he said, touching his chest. 'So something's gone wrong, right?'

'I think so,' I said, squeezing his hand.

'Did they tell you that I was dying, young Dani?'

No one has ever called me 'young Dani' since.

I looked at him, and realized that there are times in your life when you have to lie and times when you have to tell the truth.

'Yes. They said that you're going to die.'

It was one of those moments when you have to tell the truth. I knew that if I'd lied he wouldn't have believed me.

'Thank you,' he said calmly, 'thank you, young Dani.'

He turned his head to look at the table. It was as if he knew what he was going to find there, as though he had already sensed it. He saw his belongings out of the corner of his eye.

'So you know all about my life now?'

'I tried to find out what I could.'

'I like you.' His eyes half-closed again, and then suddenly blinked open. 'Do you know what those are photos of?'

'They're lighthouses, aren't they?'

He laughed, I don't know why. But quickly his laugh turned into a cough.

I hate when laughter turns into coughing or crying. When the emotional tune of our bodies changes key, all of a sudden, and it's out of our control.

He stopped coughing.

'Would you pass me the photos?'

I let go of his hand for a moment. I handed him the photographs and the letters, and immediately took hold of his fingers again.

Feeling his hand in mine was all that was keeping me from breaking down.

The situation was overwhelming, intense.

'They aren't lighthouses. They are each a part of me,' he said as he looked lovingly at the photographs. 'Reflections of what I see.' He paused. 'I have fixed the lenses on the lights of all these lighthouses; that's what I did for many, many years.'

He paused to take a deep breath, but soon he started speaking again.

'Whenever I saw any of them, it would give me the same pleasure, as though I was seeing a child of mine. Each one is like a son who always keeps an eye on you, who's always trying to keep other people safe. Going into a lighthouse was like feeling the lighthouse's stomach, or touching its throat. Inside lighthouses is where I've felt most myself in the whole universe.'

He closed his eyes again.

I didn't want to lose him. I held his hand with all the strength I could manage.

'I'm here, young Dani,' he said with a slight smile. 'Where were we?'

'You were telling me about your lighthouses.'

'My lighthouses, that's right,' he said, but added nothing. He seemed about to fall back to sleep.

'And what about the adjectives written on the back of

the pictures, on the back of all the lighthouses?' I asked, to make him keep talking. 'Is that how you felt when you saw them?'

He smiled again. 'No.' There was a long pause. 'It's how *they* felt. How I imagined they felt.'

He took a few of the photos, and started to turn them over slowly, one by one, and tell me about them.

'Some of them were old, or sad. Some were happy, lucky, useful. Most of them were tired. I fixed them and I always stayed to spend the night. I would pat their flanks from the outside, put my ear against them, listen to everything they had to tell me. They have saved so many lives.'

I looked at him. I knew that these lighthouses were not alive, but he spoke about them so directly and so clearly that he almost made me doubt it.

I looked at him; he was looking back at me, waiting for my verdict. I didn't want to say he was right just because he was dying. That wouldn't have been fair.

'Lighthouses aren't alive, Mr Martin,' I said.

He said nothing. He looked at me for a long time.

'What does it mean to be alive?' he asked me.

I hate it when people ask you questions that you know are absurd, trick questions, questions that don't have any real answer. I didn't say anything.

'Being alive is . . . is giving life,' he answered himself. 'Giving life to those who surround you. Anything that gives life is alive. Remember that. Imagine the lives that these lighthouses have saved, the lives that they have stopped from sinking into the sea.'

Suddenly he smiled. I think he must have been remembering something personal that meant 'giving life' to him.

'I fell in love with a shop mannequin when I was seventeen.' He laughed so loudly that three ICU nurses turned to look at him.

'It was a wonderful mannequin. Every day, at three in the afternoon, I passed by the shop window where it – where she – stood, and admired her poise, the elegant way she wore her clothes, the way she looked at the passers-by, and how her tranquillity dominated the whole window. I was so much in love with her that I couldn't just stand and look at her from the outside. I turned eighteen and I got a job in the shop itself. And then I was able to look after her, to protect her from the customers who wanted to buy her clothes, who thought that it would be those clothes in particular that would suit them best. Rest assured, I never removed a single item; no one did. I wouldn't allow it. It would've been humiliating for her to be naked in her window.'

He smiled, but I noticed a certain sadness, a kind of longing in his face.

'You know something, young Dani? Every night after I closed the shop, I would put on a song and we would dance together. This was our moment, our time together. She was alive, because she gave me life.' He looked straight at me. 'There's a code you can live by, one that'll make you endlessly happy. Do you dare to hear it?'

I was surprised. I hadn't expected a question like that, not after all the talk of patting the flanks of lighthouses and dancing with shop dummies after hours.

Now he was the one holding my hand tightly. Ever so tightly.

'Do you want to hear the code, young Dani? Do you dare to find out a set of rules that will bring you unlimited happiness?'

Before I could say 'yes', the nurse arrived to tell me that I had to leave, visiting hours were over.

I protested, a little. I was not so aggressive back then, and I knew that Mr Martin needed to rest.

As I left the ICU with all his precious objects in my hands, I felt scared that my future happiness would die with him. Scared that he would never tell me the code, scared that I would be lost.

Everything That Once Was Love

'Fasten your seat belt.'

The stewardess was so keen on ensuring my safety that she jolted me out of my reverie about the man who held the key to my eternal happiness.

Safety versus happiness. I had the lighthouse-monocle in my hand.

This time, my pleading had had the desired effect: perhaps the security guard had felt a little bit of sympathy; maybe he, too, had a Mr Martin in his life.

But I didn't manage to get rid of her perfume; after the lighthouse victory I couldn't ask him to do me another favour. Her scent was now stowed in the overhead locker and I could even smell it, faintly.

Maybe the fact that I hadn't yet lost it was a sign that it still wasn't the right moment for me to let go.

I held on to the lighthouse tightly, just as I had held Mr Martin's hand so many years ago.

I decided that it was time to work. There was a missing child to be found. In less than two hours, his father would want to ask me a huge number of questions, and I would need to have answers ready for each one.

On the way to the runway, I logged on to my phone email and downloaded the dossier that the father had sent me.

I smiled. Technology still fascinated me.

'You have to turn off your mobile phone.'

Policemen disguised as stewardesses fascinate me too.

I needed to see the child's face before we took off; it would help me a great deal in preparing the case, but the woman didn't walk away from my seat.

I wanted to see his face because I needed to connect with him. I could always completely understand kids who had gone missing, right from the moment I saw their faces. They always reminded me of how I looked when I ran away from home, and it would always give me strength for the search.

I thought again about what George had said about getting lost when you're young, so that you don't lose your way once you've grown up. I didn't feel like he'd got it right at all, in that moment: I had been lost as a child, but now, here I was, older, and completely lost again.

I turned off my phone.

The stewardess walked off, pleased with her petty victory.

We were about to take off. Unconsciously, I felt around the inside pocket of my jacket. I always did this before travelling in a plane, car or boat.

I was relieved to feel the little black bag I kept the rings in. There used to be only one, but now there were two.

One was my father's. I took it off his hand on the day of

the funeral. I've never worn it. My father was called Mikel, but with the years some of the engraving inside the ring had worn off and all you could read was 'Mi'.

Mi, my. My father, my fate, my ring, my strength.

But I felt that I still wasn't worthy of wearing it. When my father wore the ring, it shone, he was so strong.

The other ring was one that my former girlfriend had given me on the day she loved me most of all. I know you'll probably find it hard to believe that I know the exact day that her love for me reached its peak. But I do.

I promise that, when a relationship ends, you just know which day was the day that your love was at its highest point. You can see it, feel it.

I suppose that while you're travelling along a road, it's difficult to see all the highs and lows, but once the journey is over, you can look back and see everything clearly.

I still need to explain our relationship to you, as I promised. I should tell you about her, about how we met, how she captivated me, about all the mistakes I made, why I made them and how they ended up killing off what had once been love. Everything that was once love.

George told me one time that it's impossible to understand a relationship unless you've seen a couple argue, make love and fall asleep together.

Arguing, loving, falling asleep together.

The plane took off and I held the two rings tight; they made me feel that nothing could go wrong. They contained within them the strength of the two people I had loved most in my life.

I was sorry not to have seen a photograph of the vanished child; I wanted to be transported back to my own days as a lost boy.

After take-off, I decided to close my eyes, escape from the flight and remember a little more about my days with George.

You Learn to Fall Before
You Learn to Walk

After take-off, I went back in my mind to the moment that the boat docked in Capri.

George lifted the punch bag and slung it over his shoulder. I was scared that his prosthetic leg would give way under the weight of that enormous bag which, only minutes before, I had been hitting with immense anger.

'Are you worried that I'll fall?' he asked as he made his way down a gangway that would be difficult to negotiate even if you weren't carrying anything.

'A little bit,' I said, moving away from him just in case he did collapse.

'I've never fallen down. Don't worry, before they taught me to walk with the leg, they taught me how to take a fall.'

'They taught you to fall before they taught you to walk?' I asked, curious.

'Yes, and that's how I managed to get over any fear of falling. And if you aren't scared of falling, you walk better, and maybe even dare run every now and then. Life should be like that. Fall first, walk later.'

I smiled and moved towards him again. I wanted him to know that I trusted him to keep his footing.

'How old were you when you lost it?' I asked.

'The same age as you when you decided to run away.'

He didn't turn to look at me, but I could sense an ironic half-smile.

I got cross. 'I'm not running away. I told you that already,' I insisted.

'In that case, what's happened?'

'I just left,' I said firmly.

He didn't ask any more questions. We walked on in silence for half an hour.

We climbed up steep slopes, turned tight corners, walked along wide streets. And he never changed his pace, always walking at the same speed, always with the same rhythm.

Finally, we reached a little white house.

The door was open. He didn't use a key.

We went inside and he took the punch bag down a flight of steps. I stayed waiting for him at the door.

I wondered whether I should leave. It was a fleeting thought that came to me as I stood there, abandoned for a moment.

But I didn't leave; I knew I still had a lot to learn from him. And, to be honest, I didn't want to be alone.

He came back a few seconds later, walking just as fast as when he had been carrying the bag.

We made our way into the heart of the house. What seemed to me to be its centre of gravity. The whole place was very dark.

He opened the main windows and an amazing balcony

suddenly appeared. I'd been wrong: this was the true centre of the house.

I went out on to the terrace, enchanted by the incredible views of the Capri coast.

I hadn't realized that by climbing so many hills we had in fact ascended a great deal, until we were extremely high up, way above sea-level.

Sometimes, life is the same: the difficulty of the climb makes you forget that you are constantly progressing, constantly moving upwards.

I looked out at this picture-postcard view of Capri and realized all at once how lucky I was.

Suddenly I saw that one side of the coast was crowned by a huge lighthouse. The sight of it struck me at once, even though it was a good distance away.

It wasn't just any lighthouse. It was one I knew well. It was the magical lighthouse that had led me to run away to this island in the first place.

I hunted around in my pocket and found the silver lighthouse with the monocle on top. I looked at it secretly; I didn't want George to know anything about it. Then I looked at the full-size version.

They were basically identical: one was small and made of silver; the other was huge and seemed to be made of gold. The giant one in front of me; and the dwarf version in my hand.

Mr Martin had told me that this lighthouse, the one on Capri, was his favourite one. That was why he'd had the model made, why he'd immortalized it in metal.

I needed to remember Mr Martin, remember the things he taught me, remember his world.

I looked at George and knew that I needed for the two of them to come together, here, in this moment that I was enjoying so much. A moment when, for once, I was exactly where I was supposed to be.

'Do you have a camera?' I asked.

He nodded and went off to look in a drawer in the main kitchen table. Always drawers, the things we choose to keep in drawers.

He returned with it, and I saw that it was a traditional camera with film in it.

'I love developing film.' It was almost as if he were justifying himself, but I thought that he was boasting. 'The delay, the lack of immediacy.'

'You develop your own photos?'

'Yes, and I can show you how if you want.' He handed the camera over to me. 'Take your time with the photo, there are only two exposures left on this film. Do you want to take a picture of the bay?'

'No.'

I took the camera and focused on him. He looked down. The lighthouse was in the background, out of focus. Proud. The lighthouse fitted exactly into the viewfinder.

I tried to get them both in focus. It was difficult.

In the end, taking my time as he advised me, I managed to get both of them in the frame, and in focus. I felt proud too, now.

I knew that, once the photo was in my hands, I would

write either 'lucky' or 'proud' on the back. Both adjectives would work. But I already knew which word was the right one, the one Mr Martin would have chosen.

George took the camera once I'd taken the photo, and took one of me, also with the lighthouse in the background.

He always knew what was happening, what I was thinking.

He took the shot so quickly that I had no time to smile or pull any kind of face.

As soon as he had taken the picture, the automatic wind-back began. It was as if the film were laughing with pleasure at finally retreating back into its shell.

When I heard the noise, I realized that it had been a very long time since I'd heard it last.

'We should call your parents,' he said, breaking the silence, breaking the moment. 'They'll be worried about you.'

'I don't have any parents,' I said bluntly.

His face fell. 'Well, maybe there's someone else in your family who cares for you, loves you.'

I liked the little pause he gave between 'care for' and 'love'. Perhaps that meant something in his world.

'No; no one,' I replied.

I wasn't lying. It had been years since my brother had loved me, years since he had looked after me. If George had said 'someone in your family to put up with you and tolerate you', then maybe he would have been closer to the mark.

The sun started to set, as it tends to do at that time of day.

He looked at me intently. 'Have you seen *The Big Country*?' he asked, changing the subject suddenly.

'Is it a film?' I guessed.

He smiled and laughed. 'It is *the* film.'

He came over to me and touched me for the first time.

He put his hand lightly on my shoulder. 'You'll like it. It's about someone who fights against everything. And it's about how big the world is and how small we are. Would you like to see it?'

I didn't know. He insisted.

'We can watch it while we're eating, then I'll develop the film from the camera.'

I still wasn't sure. He carried on.

'There are photos on this film taken almost seven years ago. I really want to see them; I've waited too long. But I'd like to see something truly magnificent first of all. If something is mythical, its magic grows every time you see it.'

I looked at him. 'Seven years?'

'Yes.'

'Why didn't you develop them sooner? They'll be ruined.'

'Maybe. But I didn't have anything else to take photographs of. And I didn't want to leave those last two frames black. It's a film with only twenty-four exposures; it should be used up completely.' He paused. 'Also, it's hard for me to think about these photos; I lost the person in them a long time ago.'

A silence fell, so deep that I couldn't break it.

He looked out at the coast, and I looked at him. It was the opposite of the boat, when he looked at me while I looked at the punch bag.

A good ten minutes went by.

Eventually, I decided to come to his rescue. 'Is that film really as good as you say it is?'

I had rescued him.

'It's the best.' His face brightened. 'Here, I've got a suggestion: you stay here for three days, I'll show you how to train, how to make yourself strong; we'll watch a classic movie every evening and develop the photos, slowly. Eight photos each evening.'

'And then?' I asked. 'After the three days are up?' I could guess the answer, but I wanted to hear it from him.

'Then you'll have to go back. But the important thing is that we'll make the world stand still for these three days.'

'We'll make the world stand still?'

He nodded.

He touched me for the second time, again laying his hand on my shoulder. He patted my head. 'Have you ever made the world stand still before?'

'What does that mean?'

'It means making a conscious decision to leave the world behind, just for a little bit. To improve yourself and improve the world at the same time. To make yourself move better, and the world move better, when you come back to it. You have to make sure that no one and nothing causes you any problems during that time. Read good books, watch good movies, and above all, enjoy good conversation with someone who inspires you. And you know what?'

'What?' I said, excited and intrigued.

'Then the world gives you a reward. The universe moves in favour of those who move it. And the ones who move it are the ones who know how to make it stand still. Do you want to move the world, or do you want the world to move you?'

'I want to move it,' I said decisively. 'I want to move it!'

He came and sat next to me and started to chant along with me: 'I want to move it! I want to move it!'

And we did move it. We moved it by making it stand still.

14

A Hopeful Hand and a Blank Cheque

It was on the plane bound for Naples that I realized that I hadn't stopped the world ever since stopping it with George all those years ago.

I don't know why I paid so little attention to what he taught me, so little as to appear to have forgotten it.

Because the truth is that I believed in him, and I learnt so much when he taught me to stop the world.

But perhaps I gave up stopping the world because I couldn't find someone to do it with.

George told me that you needed two people to stop the world. That a single person would never be strong enough to stop it by himself.

The aeroplane landed, showing that the world hadn't – this time – stopped turning.

As soon as we landed, I switched on my phone and looked at the face of the vanished child. He was almost ten years old and there was a liveliness, an extraordinary happiness, in his eyes.

Parents always send the best photographs of their children, the ones where they look cutest, happiest, healthiest, but I need the other photos, the ones where they're sad or angry or a little upset.

A child's face changes so much with his emotions, and if you don't have the right photo, you can even risk finding the wrong child.

He had disappeared two days ago. Or rather, he'd been kidnapped, according to all the extra paperwork the father had sent me.

He'd included the letter that the supposed kidnapper had sent him.

I didn't read it, I never read them; I wanted to meet the parents first, go to the kid's school, see his room. Before you see the end of the film, you have to watch the beginning.

You have to understand the child, then his parents, and, only then, the alleged kidnapper.

The police hadn't yet been informed. Parents almost always respect the conditions set by their son's captors.

But after seventy-two hours they'd give in and call. This is the maximum length of time that any parent can go without their children, before they call out everywhere for them.

According to the father, the child had left school at five and hadn't come home. No one saw him getting into any suspicious cars. There were no other clues.

The story began like so many others: a child vanishing off the surface of the earth, apparently without a trace. They always start like this.

Well, I've always thought that this isn't quite the case. A

child doesn't simply disappear. He leaves or he's taken. There's no other option. And if he goes, it's because he's having a pretty shitty time.

The worst part of my job is when I find out that the missing child really has been taken, and that it'll be almost impossible to find him. Sometimes this happens. I'm not infallible.

There are people like that, people in this world who kidnap children, who imprison and abuse them.

I can't even begin to describe how much I hate them. When I come across one, in a case, I feel like killing him. I have to hold myself back, though I know that the time may come when I can't, when I'll do something crazy.

There are no limits to my hatred of anyone who would rob a child of his childhood. It is one of the worst crimes imaginable. The theft of innocence.

The child's father was waiting for me outside the airport.

I knew it was him as soon as I saw him: he didn't have to wear any special clothes or carry a card with my name on it. His eyes were his ID card. They were so tired. He hadn't slept the whole time his son had been missing.

He held out his hand to greet me; he was holding a cheque in it. The hand was hopeful, outstretched; the cheque was blank.

'You can write down whatever sum you want. It's all yours if you find my son,' was the first thing he said to me.

I took his hand, but gave him back the cheque. I didn't need any special incentives.

My goal was always the same: to find the child. Afterwards, I charged whatever I thought was fair, and it was never too much, never exploitative.

I would be no better than the man who had taken his son away, if I took advantage of a situation like this.

I tried to be as cool, as distant as possible. In my line of work it is important to seem cold. Keeping expectations to an appropriate level is one of the key lessons I have learned.

We got into his car. It was a very expensive model.

When we started up, I felt for the bag with the rings in it again. I kept my eyes on the father. It was difficult for him to drive; maybe he hadn't done so for a while. He must have had a driver, but for some reason hadn't wanted to bring him today. He probably hadn't told anyone about the disappearance, not even his closest companions.

I looked at his eyes again. They were puffy from lack of sleep and from tears. Tears and tiredness are a powerful combination for making eyes swell up.

'I'll do everything I can,' I assured him.

I was surprised to find myself saying this out loud. I don't know why I spoke. Perhaps it was because of my own recent break-up, or because his eyes reminded me so much of my own, back when I was ten years old and lost Mr Martin.

I cried so much for him. The next day, the day after I'd left him in the ICU, the nurse came and told me that he had got worse and didn't have much time left.

I was wrung out by the thought that Mr Martin was

dying slowly in the ICU, especially as I knew I was the only person in the world who was worried about him.

The worst thing of all was that they wouldn't let me see him, because I had to have my operation too, and I wasn't allowed to have any visitors, or make any visits.

I cried and cried in the empty room that we never shared.

I was terrified that he'd die. I was scared of losing him and scared that he would never tell me the secret code that meant you could be happy.

It's a peculiar kind of hopelessness that you feel when you lose someone before you really get to know them. Every time someone opened the door to my hospital room, I thought it would be the nurse coming from Mr Martin to find me.

But she never came. In the days that I didn't see him, they removed my tonsils, I recovered, and I went through all his belongings again.

I ended up almost knowing his collection of lighthouses by memory; as if they were stickers in a treasured child-hood collection. I even had my favourites, and had all the different lighthouses organized by country.

In the end, after two days with no news, when I had already lost hope and was about to go home, the nurse came to my room.

In the car with the lost boy's father, I decided to go back once again to that moment in my childhood. I needed to escape from the father's sadness for a while, at least until we were at his home and I could look around his son's bedroom.

I glanced at his eyes again, and realized that there are endless similarities between any pair of desolate, abandoned eyes.

His gaze was the perfect vehicle to take me back into my own past.

15

My Second ICU

The second time I set foot in the ICU, I did not go in hesitantly, little by little: I rushed in all of a hurry, scared that I'd get thrown out.

I ran over to where I'd last seen Mr Martin, but there was no one there. Just an empty bed with the mattress placed up on its side. I hate that they always prop them up like that; it's such an impersonal sign that the worst has happened.

And I feared the worst. The nurse looked at me with the face of someone who doesn't want to be the bearer of bad news, but who knows that there's something that has to be said.

'He's in the wing over there, with the most serious cases,' she said, making no effort to soften the blow.

I didn't know that there was a wing specifically for the most serious cases in the ICU. I thought that just being in the ICU was serious enough. I didn't realize that the patients got split up into various levels of severity.

But, as the years have gone by, I've learned that there is always a point lower than the lowest point, and one above the highest.

The nurse took me over to a closed door. It gave me the sense that this part of the hospital was kept completely separate from the rest of the building, isolated from people's eyes and ears.

I suppose no one wants to see another person die, even if you are on the cusp of death yourself.

I opened the door, and saw that there were six or seven patients in the ward. The last one I saw was Mr Martin.

He had three times as many cables and tubes connected to him as he had done the last time I saw him. The whole paraphernalia helped him to breathe, kept his heart going, and sent various substances into his body while taking various other substances out.

He winked at me. It gave me hope that I wouldn't break down.

I walked over to where he lay. I stood next to him, very close. I felt him breathing: his breath came out weakly, much weaker than the last time I'd heard it.

'Have they operated on you? Are you all right?' he asked.

'Yes, I'm fine, Mr Martin.'

He smiled and touched my neck just where my tonsils had once been.

'What about you?'

He waved a hand vaguely, as if to say, 'Well, this is how things are.'

Such a gesture really does exist, it encompasses everything I've explained to you.

I put his things on his bedside table once again. This table was much smaller. I suppose that when death is getting closer, tables also diminish a little. You've got nearly nothing you need to keep with you, so you don't need that much space.

He smiled when he saw the photographs of the lighthouses and the envelopes with the lists of numbers in them.

'Do you know what those numbers mean?'

I shook my head. I would have found it too difficult to speak. I was terrified that he would die at any moment.

'My father was a poker player.' His voice was very weak, but it was still just about audible. 'Ever since I was a young boy, people would come to play at our house every night. They came with cigars and drink, and they'd spend eight or ten hours at a stretch playing poker in the lounge. I slept in the lounge. On a sofa in one corner. My father made me sleep there so that he could keep an eye on me while he kept the other on his cards. He loved poker as much as he loved me. He was a great man. And he had lost his wife too soon, so he didn't want to lose his son's childhood as well. I always watched him admiringly while he played. I was so excited to watch their poker games, with all their different rules and shades of meaning, and so many different emotions. I saw some people who won, some who lost. Night after night, luck passing from one hand to the other and back again. In the end, from looking at these people for so long, from living their victories and defeats along with them each night, I ended up knowing, even with my eyes closed, who was bluffing, who had a terrible hand, who had a royal flush. And it was all down to the way they breathed, or how they lit their cigarettes, or even just a little change in the way they spoke or bid. They were tiny, almost imperceptible details, but they were a part of the soundtrack to my sleep and I could tell between them almost as easily in my dreams as when I was awake. I became an expert and every now and then I helped my father to win. Ever since I was seven years old, I've been in love with gaming, playing cards, gambling. I never call it "gambling"; to me it's just "life". Life with elements of chance in it, but then again, isn't life always filled with elements of chance, young Dani?'

I nodded my head gently. I couldn't take my eyes off him. He'd stopped looking tired and now seemed flushed with enthusiasm, even passion.

'When I was older, I started to play poker myself,' he continued. 'But that was his game. I could never be better than my father. He taught me everything, but I never managed to become a master. Spades, hearts, diamonds and clubs were his passion, but not mine. But he taught me a rule that is easily adaptable to almost any game. "Only bet what you don't need." That's the most important thing to know, so that you don't ruin your life or the lives of those around you. "Never break that rule, never," he would insist, over and over again. When I was ten years old, I would bet half my pocket money; when I was twenty, it was half my salary. But I never lost control; I always stuck to betting only what I didn't need, the rest was for living. My father also taught me that the pleasure you get from winning should never be greater than the pleasure you get from losing. It can be pleasurable to lose, because it makes you understand the value of winning all the more. And, as time goes by, losses are always transformed into gains.'

He stopped breathing for a few seconds. It was as if he had simply turned off, but before I could go and look for someone to help, he carried on speaking as though nothing had happened. It was pretty bleak.

'I spent ten years looking for my game, the one I could master. My father told me that everybody has one, one that suits them better than all the others and gets their adrenaline going in a way that's just pure pleasure. Poker was never my game, neither was blackjack; nor was greyhound racing or horse racing. I didn't get any kicks from the lottery or the football pools. And then she appeared, and with her, the game of my life.'

He hunted around in the envelopes stuffed full with lists of numbers. It was difficult because his hands were covered with tubes and cables, but he didn't give up until he found what he was looking for.

One of the envelopes had within it, as well as its list of numbers, a photograph of a woman. I don't know how I'd missed it.

In the photo, the girl was dressed in a strange set of clothes, almost like a uniform. The snapshot had been taken outside a castle.

She was smoking, her gaze lost in the distance. Tall and elegant, she looked a little bit like a shop mannequin, or at least that's how it seemed to me.

'I took the photo while she was on a break.' He smiled

and, for the first time, I saw his teeth. 'The employees were allowed to leave the casino every hour to have a cigarette. I always stopped playing at the same time and went out so that I'd get to see her. I loved to look at her from far away. I suppose it must be because I usually had her so close to me, just a few inches away every single night. She was the chief of the team that ran the roulette wheel in a casino that they'd set up in this lovely castle, which you can see behind her. I'd never found roulette appealing at all, not until I saw her working the wheel. She threw the ball so elegantly and spun the wheel with such enthusiasm that just the sound it made was almost addictive. I swear that when it was her turn to be there, people bet three times what they usually would. I stayed next to her. I watched her, I smelt her scent, I felt her near me and, every now and then, I gave her a couple of chips to put on seventeen and nineteen. Those were my first two lucky numbers; then they changed. And much later they changed again.'

The nurse came in with some medicine and he paused his story for a few minutes. I think that he didn't want just anyone to hear what he had to say. It made me feel very important.

When she left, I couldn't help myself from asking the question that had been running through my head ever since he had started the story.

'And did you marry her?'

He laughed and coughed in almost equal measure. This time it didn't bother me so much.

'I never even spoke to her. Never. I looked at her

hundreds of times from up close and thousands of times from far away. When they moved her to a new casino, I followed her to the place they had sent her and carried on with the same routine. Near and far, the woman observed and desired. And over the years, the feelings I had for her made their way into the game. I channelled all my love into the game of roulette. Every time her hand touched the ball, I felt her magic. It was a way of making love to her, of feeling that we were doing something together. And so it was that I found my game, my passion, the one thing that gave me true pleasure. And from that point onwards, everything spun out of control and I became a roulette professional.'

Mr Martin opened a couple more envelopes, took out a bunch of papers with numbers scribbled all over them, and showed them to me.

'Every sheet of paper is a roulette wheel in a particular casino. The numbers in red are the winning numbers. If you play these numbers you will always win, whatever the hour, whatever the day or time of year.'

I was a little surprised by his confidence. I'd never played roulette before, but surely it couldn't be quite that simple?

'It's impossible. You can't know the numbers that are going to come up, and even if you did, when they changed the wheels the numbers would change as well, wouldn't they?' I asked.

'No.' He smiled. 'I have been in so many casinos that I can assure you that the important thing is not the wheel but the ground it's standing on. Gravity and chance make sure that there will always be lucky numbers,' he said, entirely sure of himself.

He gathered all the envelopes and gave them to me. 'They're for you; they're worth a lot of money. I want you to take them, young Dani, and only use them when you really need to.'

I took the heap of crumpled paper, not really knowing what to say. Nothing in my life so far had given me any desire to enter the world of gambling.

'And what about her?' I asked. 'Did she die?'

He took a long time to answer. A very long time.

'I lost sight of her a few years ago. I have spent my life looking for her.'

'To tell her how you felt?'

'No.' He smiled so much this time that you could see his gums. 'Just to see her, from close up and from far away. There are people in this world, young Dani, who nourish you – just the sight of them nourishes you. You don't need any more than that. They give you energy.'

Energy. The same idea that George would share with me, only a few years later. But back then, I didn't really get what Mr Martin was saying about roulette, or the mysterious girl, or her energy.

I thought he was going to show me how to be happy, and instead he'd just told me about gambling addictions and how he'd been a coward in the face of love.

I didn't say what I thought out loud, but he read my mind again.

'Happiness doesn't really exist, Dani.' This was one of the few times that he didn't call me 'young Dani'. 'All that exists is the chance that you have, every day, to be happy that day. If you think about happiness as a global idea, everything collapses under its own weight. Look out of the window.' He pointed towards a tiny glass pane that looked onto the street.

I went over to it. I was shocked that the serious cases didn't have huge windows to look out of; they needed them, to be able to say goodbye to the world.

'Do you see all those people walking around meaninglessly, each of them heading in their own direction, on their own personal journey?' he asked.

I looked at them. I don't know how he knew they were there. From where he was lying he couldn't see down to the street.

'I see them,' I said.

'Do you realize that they're all going somewhere, for some reason? Neither you nor I would change places with them for anything. And that's because we like our lives, our paths, the faces that we show the world. We don't know where they're going, what they need to do. But at night, everything changes. Look at the tallest buildings at dawn and see how few lights there are in them, how very few. Nearly everyone is asleep; there are only one or two who are awake. Those are the ones who are searching, the ones who are making discoveries. At that moment, when almost everyone is asleep, they are falling in love or enjoying deep conversations. And these feelings and these words will change their lives. Young Dani, always make sure that there are more nights in your life than days. And if you are ever lost and don't know where to go, always ask yourself the most important question: "What might someone else do, if they were me?"'

We were silent for a few seconds. He seemed to pause once again. This time it took him a lot longer to come back. It was clear that he had very little left in him.

I said his name out loud, three times, but he didn't come back. I squeezed his hand, hard, but it had no effect.

Finally I tried carrying on the conversation as though nothing had happened. 'What would someone else do if they were me?' I repeated.

And then he came back, as though talking about all this had revitalized him somehow. Speaking seemed to give him strength.

'Yes, exactly. Find another person you share energy with and ask them what they would do if they could live your life for a day or so. What would they change about it? How would they do their hair? What would they eat? What would they do? How would they live your life if they had control of your body for two days?'

'And does it work?'

'Of course.' He smiled. 'I've tried it a thousand times and it always gives me the strength to carry on. But you need to find someone to do it with, and that's not easy. The person has to be special, and has to know how to look at things from the outside, to give you another perspective on your life, when you are lost.'

I looked at him several times, unable to take all this in. He switched off for another moment. His breathing slowed down after this last sentence, his vital signs disappeared and all the machines attached to him started to buzz and beep.

I knew what I should ask him to make him come back at once.

'Shall we gamble together?'

His breathing started up again, the machines stopped calling out. I knew this would not last long. I was losing him.

He looked at me with absolute affection. He passed his hand over my face, my mouth, my neck and my hands. 'I'd love to, young Dani. But my time is up.'

He paused, I thought perhaps for good. But he still had something left to tell me. He looked at the lighthouse-monocle, then took it and pressed it into my hand.

'It's for you, so you don't forget me. It's a lighthouse in Capri. I fell for it, it became my favourite son. When you find the photo I took of it, you'll see that on the back I've written "magic". It is a magical place and when you go there you'll feel its magic. If you have problems, if you ever have problems, go to it and it will take care of you. The dark monocle is to let you look at clouds. I worked in the film business for a while and I was the man whose job it was to find out when the clouds would go away and the sun would come back. They needed me to make sure they were always filming with the same kind of light, so that the picture didn't get brighter and darker within scenes. I was good at that. I've always been good at everything to do with clouds and lighthouses and the sea and the sun and the wind. If you look through the monocle and look at a cloud, then you'll be able to see the sun behind it and work out the wind speed, and how long it will take for the cloud to pass and the sun to shine again. I had them put together, because the lighthouse is magical, and being able to guess when the sun will return is magical as well. Remember, if one day you find you are in need of a little magic, then go to Capri.'

It was getting harder and harder for him to breathe. The machines all started to buzz and beep like mad things.

I called for the nurse at the top of my voice. Mr Martin was leaving, and I was sad and scared.

Suddenly Mr Martin looked straight at me, calling me over to him with his eyes. I put my ear to his mouth and he said three or four words that I couldn't quite catch.

He said them several times, always with the same rhythm. The same intensity. It was a message for me, but I didn't understand it; he wasn't speaking intelligibly at all.

The message came to an end and Mr Martin left me.

I looked at him and suddenly felt an energy entering into my body, an energy that filled me with calm and peace. It was as if his energy were leaving him and coming to share my body.

Doctors and nurses tried, unsuccessfully, to bring him back to life. But I knew that he'd already gone.

I squeezed his hand as tightly as I could, said thank you, and kissed him on the cheek.

16

You Do Not Understand
Other People's Tears

I was crying again, in the car, sitting next to a man who was almost a complete stranger.

I just found it impossible to remember Mr Martin without bursting into tears. I remember the son of a dancer once saying to me that people either burst out laughing or burst into tears, and that it's always worth it, letting those two emotions explode.

The child's father looked at me in surprise. My sadness was too much for him. But he didn't say a word. It's so hard to understand other people's tears if you don't know the story behind them, if you don't have the facts.

I think it was only then I realized that it was because of Mr Martin that I'd started my life's work searching for missing children.

Somehow, the first time I lost myself wasn't when I got on that boat to Capri, but there in the ICU, flooded with tenderness and passion.

Mr Martin was a passionate man, a man who loved impossible things. I was lucky to have met him, lucky that my ten-year-old body and mind weren't taken away from me by some depraved or evil man, some perverted son of a bitch. Instead I met a great soul who tried to teach me the importance of being different. There are very few people in the world who don't give in, who refuse to lead mediocre lives.

I've chosen to look for children who have gone missing; I think this is my way of escaping from the path of convention, of mediocrity.

And I think I'm pretty good at it, because my childish side and my dwarfish side help me to really understand them, to connect with them and their problems. It's like connecting with my own lost self, and that brings me close to their essence.

I glanced across at the father and saw that he was itching to tell me everything he could. He needed to feed me all the data he had, he needed to feel useful. But I also knew that if he did, it would prime me to see things a certain way: that I'd end up understanding the father, instead of the son.

I avoided meeting his gaze. But I knew that he'd soon start talking, because he'd looked across at me just a moment ago.

'Do you have children?'

This was only the second thing that he had said to me after all that nonsense about the cheque, and it was the worst possible thing he could have come out with. The question was so deeply tangled up with my break-up, with my ex-girlfriend and with our biggest problem together. Me and her and the children we had wanted.

I know I should tell you about her. I've been holding

back information about my break-up – its reasons, its causes – for quite some time now.

But I have to tell you about George first, or else you won't understand me, where I'm coming from.

I wish we could always try to understand people before judging them. And I wish people were capable of being honest and just telling us about themselves, letting us understand them before we form an opinion.

'I don't have any children.' I had to give him an answer.

'He's my only child,' the father explained.

He didn't say anything else because, worked up now, he had started to sob. I knew that I should calm him down somehow, before I let myself head back into my memories again. It was the only fair thing to do: you can't just head off and live in the past while someone is suffering in the present, right next to you. Also, sympathy and understanding were a part of the job.

'There's no reason to fear that anything bad has happened to him,' I said. 'The fact that someone has kidnapped him doesn't mean that anyone is actually going to hurt him. Lots of people –'

He interrupted me, furious. 'Have you even read the dossier I sent you?' he yelled.

I shook my head.

'I am a judge. I specialize in cases of paedophilia and child abuse. I've sent more than a hundred paedophiles to prison!' He was shouting louder than I'd shouted at the security guard in the airport. 'Don't tell me that it'll all be all right because, if you'd read the letter that the kidnapper sent me, you'd have seen that the person who has kidnapped my child is a paedophile who I got sentenced to eight years in prison.'

I said nothing.

I had not been very professional. I'd let my personal life overtake my work. What the father had just told me changed everything, even though I knew that it wasn't conclusive.

Perhaps the note was a fake. Sometimes a child runs away because he isn't getting enough love. Because he sees that his father cares more about other children than about him; that can be a strong enough reason to run away and leave a forged letter behind.

I decided to stop looking his way. I knew that I'd lost a little bit of the trust he had previously placed in me.

We were coming close to the ferry that would take us over to Capri. And so the ferry would come back into my life once again. As if nothing had changed at all with the passing years.

We drove the car into the hold and I took the opportunity to think back to *The Big Country*. To the first masterpiece I had seen with George, back in the Capri of my adolescence.

I promise I'll tell you about her, about the reasons for our break-up, after I've told you about that.

17

The Intensity of an Anecdote, Brought Back to Life in Another Body

We saw *The Big Country* and George was right, I felt just like Gregory Peck. I, too, was someone trying fight against the norms of the world I lived in, against everything that was considered proper, everything that the world expected of me.

I felt all of this and I was only thirteen years old. I didn't even dare to imagine what would happen next.

I was flabbergasted by how big the Wild West was, how small the people looked against it. It reminded me a lot of how I felt, being in Capri.

It felt as if George and I were the only people living in the city. Two tiny figures on an immense island. I took a breath and felt the smallness that you always feel when faced with natural grandeur.

It was just at that moment that I realized that George and I could play 'What would you do if you were me?' George was the perfect person to try out Mr Martin's game with.

I looked straight at him. I wanted to ask him, but I was shy.

'Did you like the film?' he asked me.

'A lot.'

I looked at him again, daring to speak this time. 'Would

you like to play "What would you do if you were me?"' I asked.

He smiled. 'What is it?'

I told him everything. I told him about Mr Martin, about going into another person's world when you feel lost. About giving advice about what you would do if you were them for two days, and then leaving.

He listened and seemed to be charmed by everything he heard. And I was happy that, for the second time in my life, a grown-up was treating me like an adult.

When I finished explaining it to him, he told me that he liked the idea a great deal, but that we should get to know each other a little better first. He thought that if you were going to change the course of someone else's life, then you really had to know as much as possible about it first.

I hesitated, but I thought he was probably right.

He said that we should go and develop the photos together. 'The best way to get to know someone is to share the things they like,' he said.

I liked the sound of his suggestion, so I agreed.

His darkroom was two floors below the room where we'd been watching *The Big Country*.

We had to walk down almost fifty steps to get there. The subterranean cave smelt of the sea and its walls were solid rock. I felt I was in the heart of the island.

And the best part was that I wasn't at all scared. I was alone with a stranger in a subterranean hole that looked a bit like a dungeon, and I felt absolutely fine.

The only thing was that I was a little bit tired. I couldn't remember how long it had been since I'd last slept. I felt my body aching, but there was something in my exhaustion that I found almost pleasant.

We settled down to develop the photographs straight away. He explained the process as we worked. I had never developed anything before, and I loved the precision of the technique, the fact that you had to follow specific, extremely exact timings, and the calming glow of the single red light bulb.

'Developing film is like going fishing,' George said. 'Fishing in the knowledge that you'll eventually catch something – something that you created yourself.'

Suddenly I realized that the big red punch bag that George had carried halfway across the island was hanging in the middle of the room.

It took a while for the photos to appear. They were sunk in those strange liquids, and we were keen to see them.

My gaze flicked back and forth between the punch bag that fascinated me and the photos, and from the photos back to that fascinating hanging bag.

And then I saw something strange hanging on the wall. I couldn't see exactly what it was, because the red light of the darkroom didn't allow me to see it fully. But I sensed that something was there.

I walked over to it slowly. I felt his eyes on the back of my neck.

A few seconds later, I heard his footsteps behind me.

When I reached the wall, I could hear his breath.

It was the only moment I ever felt scared, the whole time

I was there: I swear that, before then, I hadn't felt any kind of panic at all in this place.

But, feeling him so close to me, and not knowing what it was that was hanging on the wall, made me feel a little uncomfortable, to say the least.

It's the fear that I always feel when I'm looking for children who may be in danger. The fear that gives me the strength not to throw in the towel; the fear that helps me to fight until I find them.

I've been to many of these attics, where children have been captured and kept against their will, and the worst thing is that in each one, you can feel this same fear living on in the walls, the fear of children who have been given some rough shelter there.

Children mark their territory; their infinite fear sinks into the walls.

I feel sad that this is a memory I connect with George. He never did anything bad to me and never made me feel anything other than happy. He would never have hurt me.

'Do you want to know what it is that's hanging over there on the wall?' he asked me, in a voice that immediately put me at ease.

I nodded, silently.

He reached over for the red light that hung in the middle of the room and pointed it up at the wall.

The wall lit up and I found myself face to face with a whole vast collage of Polaroid photos. They were set up in groups of twelve, divided by years. I think I must have counted almost forty years up there on the wall.

The photos were all portraits of men and women in different places, each caught in the middle of a moment of his or her different daily routine. Drinking coffee, smoking, laughing.

If I hadn't seen Mr Martin's lighthouses all those years before, I would probably have found this all a little more strange than I actually did.

But once you've already seen a huge, intriguing collection of photos, each with their own defining adjective, there's not much you'll be surprised by, photography-wise.

'Who are they?' I asked.

'My pearls.' He smiled. 'I've searched for twelve pearls every year of my life. Twelve people who I didn't know, but who appeared to me and who made their mark on my world so completely that my whole being, my whole self, turned around.'

'Your self turned around?' I repeated.

'Mr Martin was a pearl in your life.' I was grateful that he was giving me a concrete example. 'He was a jewel that the world gave you, and although several years have gone by, you still have him, you still have that jewel. That proves what a great pearl he was, because time hasn't taken away any of his brilliance or his intensity.'

I studied the wall carefully. It was impossible to tell who the predominant figures were. The pearls were people of all colours, of all sexes, of all ages. I liked looking at each of them.

I don't know how long I stood there in silence, looking at that necklace. The pearl necklace.

There was something about those faces, those gazes, that gave out energy. I smiled. 'There's energy in them, isn't there?'

He smiled as well. 'A lot of energy. Three of them are far more than pearls. They are bearers of that special energy that I spoke to you about in the boat, the energy you have to find. Souls that blend with your own soul.'

'Really?' I was thrilled by this definition.

Suddenly I remembered what had happened when Mr Martin died. Perhaps that had been his soul blending with my own. I couldn't be sure. George carried on talking.

'With time, some pearls turn into diamonds. Out of every eighty or ninety pearls you meet, one will become a diamond. A diamond is someone who becomes so essential and so important to your life, so fundamental, that it's as if they were created just for you.'

I understood what he was saying, but I think that my face must have suggested the opposite. He carried on giving me examples.

'These diamonds are like little crumbs, particles, drops of you that have been spilt.'

'Spilt?' My interest was increasing.

'Yes, I think that we all spill a little in our lifetimes.'

'What do you mean? Who spills us, how are we spilt?'

'Each of us gets spilt, and mixes with four other people. You spill out into the world and eventually you meet the other four people who form part of your mix. It's one of life's goals, to find the people who you are mixed with, to follow the signs to find them, not to let yourself be led astray.'

144

'What are the signs?' I asked.

'They're the things that connect each person in your mix with the next. It can be extremely simple.'

I thought about the Polaroid pictures. Mr Martin's, and now, George's. Perhaps these were the signs, the fragments, the diamonds, the droplets, the little broken bits of my soul.

I didn't say anything, because I thought it might be a little arrogant to believe that I'd already found two of my diamonds by the age of thirteen. But I did ask him another question.

'What happens when you find all four diamonds?'

He took his time before answering. Too much time for my liking – I was so desperate for the answer, I could barely wait.

'I don't know, but I'm sure something happens.'

I could tell that he was lying to me, but I didn't dare ask him again.

We went back to the basins, where the pictures were now bobbing about like trapped fish.

There was a woman in all of them, apart from two: the picture that he took of me, and the one that I took of him.

In one, the woman looked at him. He seemed to be smaller next to her.

George looked over the photos with a nostalgia that I will never forget: I've never seen anything quite like it, not even in the faces of people completely lost in memory.

'Is she a pearl?' I guessed.

'A diamond in the rough.' He smiled. 'She left years ago.

I haven't been brave enough to look at these photos until now.'

He stopped talking. He went over to the punch bag in the middle of the room and ran his hand over it.

'Do you know what's inside this bag?' he asked, still stroking it.

I shook my head.

'Pieces of my pearls. When someone disappears from my life, from my world, I take some piece of their clothing, or an important object that defines them, and I stuff it into the bag. There are lots of her things in here. Sometimes I hit the bag in anger, sometimes I run my hand over it, sometimes I dance with it – and, in a way, I'm dancing with her, and with the other people who have left me behind.'

He started to dance. I remembered Mr Martin and his mannequin. It was beautiful, the intensity of this anecdote, brought back to life again, moving through another body.

He danced with that bag, filled with the vestiges and memories of his pearls, the people he had loved and cherished. I felt envy: I hadn't loved anyone yet.

The music that accompanied the dance was the sound of the gently clinking hook that held the punch bag to the ceiling, and the low buzz of the red light bulb.

I felt so jealous of this man, who lived his life with such intensity. There was nothing I could do but go over and start dancing along with him.

There we were, dancing, with only this strange and beautiful red bag in the air between us.

I swear, I've never felt so wonderful dancing since. And that's coming from someone who tries to dance with everyone I feel any kind of connection with.

But the strange embrace of that red leather, the feeling of it against my skin, the knowledge of all it held within, was pure energy, energy that passed through me and every nerve in my body: energy that has never been equalled.

Every so often my fingertips and George's would lightly brush together. Sixty-three and thirteen, brought together by a punch bag. Half a century of experience dividing us.

If the police had come in at that moment, looking for me, they would have arrested George at once. Sometimes images, the way things look, can't come close to reflecting the way things feel, the way they are in reality.

It was a little like a precious mother-of-pearl paperknife, encrusted with diamonds. To the eyes of someone who didn't know any better, it might just look like a gaudy old flickknife decked out with tacky adornments.

We danced for a long time. When we'd finished dancing, I looked at him and hugged him.

'You have to go home. You know that, don't you?' he whispered.

I nodded, but my eyes were elsewhere. I was resisting what he was saying; there was so much more we had left to do.

'What about those two other films we were going to watch, and the exercises you were going to show me, and the game where you tell me what you'd do if you were me and what you would change in the three days when we stop the world?' I asked, the typical teenager who always wants everything all at once.

He smiled. 'If you want, we can watch another film before you go. And I can train you for a couple of hours.' He went on, looking for the best way to answer. 'As for the game: I'm sure you'll find someone who knows you better and more deeply than I do. And, anyway, three days could never have been as intense as those ten minutes of dancing. Intensity isn't decided by how long something lasts, but by how much emotion you feel.'

He picked up one of the photos of that mysterious woman and added it to his collage, his wall of pearls. He positioned it in the column for a few years ago.

Then he took the photo of me and added it to the column for 'today'. I was his first pearl of the year. I felt happy.

I took the photo of him and put it in my pocket. I'd found another diamond, I was sure of it.

And he kept his word. Though I never had any doubt that he would.

He trained me for the next two hours. He taught me to move my neck first of all. 'Everything passes through the neck,' he said. 'If you can move it well, then the rest of your body will move with it: it's what links the body and the mind.'

He told me about how lazy our bodies are, how bodies resist change, how they resist doing anything we try to force them to do, even something as simple as turning to face the other way.

'You have to fight against your own body, to make it understand that everything is for the best, that you're acting in its own best interests. Our body is both our worst enemy and our best friend,' he explained. 'It complains about having to make any effort, but only for the first four or five seconds. Remember this, pain is only momentary. Your body is your enemy, and it is your friend.'

Suddenly, stirred up by George's words, I said something that I'd never thought I would say out loud.

It's incredible when that happens, when you are sure you'll keep something secret for ever and ever – you promise yourself, you swear yourself to secrecy. And then, all of a sudden, you find yourself speaking out. It makes you feel strange, euphoric.

Very strange. Very euphoric.

'I'm a dwarf.'

He didn't say anything. He looked me up and down three times. 'Do you want to stop being one?' he asked me.

I was shocked by his question. But, intrigued, I decided to answer. 'Yes. I promised my mother that I would, back when she was still alive. My parents were dwarves as well. They were very happy with the way they were, but my mother had always thought that I was a giant, ever since I was inside her. One day I said, "I'll grow taller for you." And she was so happy that she got goosebumps. And I'm sure she wasn't pretending.'

The tears were pouring down my face. I hadn't even realized that I was about to cry.

George did not soften at the sight of my tears. He carried on looking at me, gravely serious, looking as if he had no sympathy for my sadness whatsoever. But actually, rather than just comforting me, he wanted to give me some advice that I would use for the rest of my life.

'There is nothing that is truly impossible in this world, young Dani. Nothing. If you want to grow, then your body will grow, because it is your ally, but in order to let it grow, you have to stand back and let the other person who lives inside you be free. You will always be a dwarf inside. A dwarf in a giant's body.'

He had called me 'young Dani'. I realized that what he had just said, the rhythm of his words, perfectly matched Mr Martin's final words, those words that I had never understood. Those sounds that Mr Martin had made again and again when he was just on the edge of death – they had the same rhythm, the same intensity as the words I had just heard from George.

It was almost like dubbing a foreign film. In his final moments, Mr Martin had spoken a strange language, a language which, it now appeared, George knew how to speak, how to translate.

'A dwarf in a giant's body.' It was strangely familiar. It was the last phrase that Mr Martin had wanted to share with me. I felt, somehow, complete.

'And who are you?' I asked.

He smiled. 'A fighter in the body of a coward.'

I didn't ask why he gave me that answer.

We made our way up to the first floor. This was the end

of my adventure. My escape, my time as a runaway, was coming to an end, that much was certain.

He gave me money for the return ferry. I gave him Mr Martin's sheet of paper with all the numbers from the roulette wheel at the Capri casino. He should bet on 12 and 21. I didn't know if he would try it out, or if it would work, but I was sure that the sheet was worth at least as much as a return trip on the ferry.

As we said goodbye, a marching band was playing in the street. There was a carnival on Capri.

Outside, we could hear them playing one of those tunes they always play on public holidays. Inside, we said our goodbyes in near-complete silence.

The contrast was marvellous and strange. Inside, subdued longing; contagious happiness outside.

I walked out of the door and followed the band down to the coast. They walked ahead and I went slowly after them. They were accompanying me; I needed them so that I wouldn't get lost.

I never saw George again. Some time later, I got a letter from a lawyer telling me that he had died. I felt a kind of sharp, stabbing sensation. It felt as if his soul was hitching up to mine. Or maybe that's just what I wanted to feel.

There was a note that George had written for me, enclosed with the letter. All it said was, 'My son is inside another son. It's yours if you want it.'

I read those lines and burst into tears. It had all happened just like he had promised and I had grown. I had grown a great deal and become the giant that my mother had always wanted me to be. But inside, as he had guessed, I was still the same little dwarf.

I remember that, when I left Capri on the ferry, I thought I would never return.

'You never need to go back to the place that has made you happy,' as the song has it. Ironically.

18

A Dwarf Comes Back as an Adult

And now I was back on Capri. The ferry pulled into the harbour. There was no punch bag to carry this time, no band that I could follow along the coast.

Twenty-seven years had gone by, and now I was looking for a lost child, instead of being the lost child myself.

I didn't want to let myself become emotional, but I couldn't help it. I'd dreamed about setting foot on this island again. I never thought that dream would come true.

The dwarf comes back as an adult. The dwarf comes back and he's now an adult.

The father hung his head low, agitated to be once again at the site of his son's disappearance, but I felt empowered by having come back to the place where I had found myself.

We went straight to his house. It was a long way away from George's; almost the furthest you could go and still be on the island.

There was a woman waiting for us at the door. She must have been almost a hundred years old. I didn't yet know that in a few hours' time, this woman would change my life by asking me one of the most intense questions I'd ever

been asked, that she would talk to me about the old *bolero*
'If You Tell Me To Come . . .'

In that moment she was simply a grandmother worried
about her missing grandson.

I said hello to her in passing, not paying much attention,
but she took my hand and gripped it with an intensity that
pulled me back through the years, back to when I was ten,
to when I was thirteen. It released an energy that pulsed
up through my fingers and into my soul.

'Find him,' she said, 'and I'll help you to find yourself.'

I didn't know what to say.

The child's father took me to one side. 'Don't pay her
any attention,' he said. 'She's sick with worry about her
grandson.'

But I believed what she had said to me. She meant it, I
knew. I knew it was true. I looked back at her as the father
walked me into the house.

In a flash, I realized the power of that island; there was
something about it that drew together my diamonds— my
essence – that helped me find myself when I was lost.

I pondered going to find George's son inside another
son, but I knew it wasn't the right time. Everything else
had to take a back seat for now: my life, my problems, my
girlfriend. The boy was the only important thing, my only
priority.

It was the only thing motivating me. I have always been
good at my job. I have been good only at my job.

'Do you really need to see his room?' the father asked
me.

'I do. It's very important that I see it. I have to. It's crucial.'

I have to. Again, those verbs – 'have to', 'must' – brought thoughts of her back to me. Where was she?

I didn't need to worry about her any more. But I still wanted to worry about her.

I've always believed that none of us have met the most important people in our lives yet – they're always just out of reach, just around the next corner. As they don't exist for us yet, we don't need to worry about whether or not they've been run over, or if one of their loved ones has died, or if they are sad, or abandoned. They don't exist in our world yet, so their sadness and happiness aren't part of it either, and don't affect us. At least, that is, until the day we meet them, and become a part of their world.

Now I realized that the same thing happens with people we've lost, people we'll never see again. It's as if we need to forget about what's happened to them, about what troubled them. But I don't want to do this; people need to survive. Perhaps I didn't want to survive myself back then.

We got to the boy's room. I felt shocked when I saw the door. His name was Izan, it said, in letters that he had stuck on it. The sight of that name was overwhelming.

I walked into the room and felt my blood run cold. It was filled with stars stuck to the ceiling and drawings of planets on the walls. It was like walking into outer space.

'Izan loves the universe,' the father said.

He loves the universe. Who doesn't? The father turned

out the light and suddenly a fluorescent spectacle shone out of the darkness.

Standing in the middle of the room, I felt myself drifting, suspended, in space. My hair stood on end; I got goosebumps, for real this time. It was all too much for me.

He was called Izan. He liked outer space. All I needed was the music.

There was an old record player in the room. I got it working and it began to play 'The Show Must Go On', that wonderful song Queen wrote to face up to their lead singer's illness. To keep on keeping on.

I know that these might all just be small coincidences, but it was all so incredible for me, three little signs that belonged to my world and to her world, the world of my ex-girlfriend.

And to the world of our son, above all.

Yes, I think that here, in this room, with the lights switched off and the whole cosmos spinning around me, I can at last tell you about our son, the reason we broke up.

Even though I don't want to admit it.

19

It Was Not a Search; It Was a Hunt

Yes, I know I told you that there were fifteen possible reasons for my break-up. And I wasn't lying to you: they were there – each one exists.

But there's always been the one major reason for our unhappiness, the main one, the one that never changed. The child was always there, throughout our thirteen years living together. I met her when I was twenty-seven.

I know I should tell you everything. It's just a little difficult for me. I don't know where to start.

I know that I'm in the room of a child who has disappeared on Capri, but it feels like I'm in the room of the child who never arrived.

We wanted to call him Izan. It was the first thing that we decided. We agreed on it almost without thinking. It was one morning in Menorca; we'd been living together for three years and we were talking about maybe having children.

We were thinking about names as we walked on the beach, approaching a lighthouse. Izan cropped up almost at once. It was incredible, we said it in unison.

And from that moment, we began to wonder what our son, what Izan, would be like.

I remember there was a strange wind blowing that day, all through the island, and we felt our thoughts, our ideas and our dreams all gathering together and blowing out to sea.

I can't remember which of us decided that it would be a good idea to stop and make a wish for the child to turn out just the way we wanted, so that a gust would carry the wish away and make it into a reality.

You know the little things that couples do together, when they're in love. I like the codes of coupledom: each one is unique. No one can steal them from you, no one can snatch them away.

I know I'm struggling to get this out; it's hard to say what I mean. But speaking about her, about our break-up, about Izan, the child who never came, the child we already loved so much, imagining in every detail what he would be like and what he would become, it all hurts me a great deal.

On the Menorca coast we dreamed up the perfect baby boy. Izan, whom we thought would come at some point in the next two years, but who never came.

That night in Menorca, she said that he would love the stars and planets, that they would be his favourite thing. That his room would be like the cosmos.

It was only a wish, made into the Menorca wind. Is it possible that the wind had travelled across the sea to Capri, that it had borne the wish along with it and made it real?

The lost boy was the same age as Izan was when we started to imagine him.

I can't remember all that we said about the imaginary child. There was so much. The last thing I remember is talking about how I wanted him to have a record player. I had hoped that he would become, like me, obsessed with 'The Show Must Go On'. It was one of my favourite songs.

We always want our children to love the worlds we have created for ourselves, even down to our taste in music. We want them to want to follow our path.

But Izan never came. Never. And that was our big problem.

We tried the traditional way first of all, but she didn't get pregnant. We tried for a couple of years and we didn't get anywhere.

And, little by little, it turned from being strange to being traumatic. As the months went by, having sex started to feel more and more like a duty, an activity with a goal: producing a baby.

We took tests, changed the hours and times when we had sex and, finally, we decided to find out where the problem really lay.

The problem. It should have been so easy to fix. There are couples who tell you that it all just happened by accident, that they weren't even looking to have a child.

Meanwhile, we didn't know where our missing child could be, and we weren't just 'looking' to have one any longer. It was no longer a search, but a hunt.

The tests came back. They said we were both fine. They told us it must be psychological.

But this diagnosis did not put us at ease. Instead we

grew obsessed. How could we be physically in perfect shape, but psychologically incapable of conceiving a child? Perhaps if it hadn't been mental, if one of us had actually been to blame physiologically, then everything would've been much easier. The guilty party, the infertile one, would have felt bad, but the other person would have done all they could to save the situation. The other person would have wanted nothing more than to save his lover, her lover. But if we were both suffering, then who would save us?

They were complicated years. Sex became a duty that we had to carry out in a particular way, followed by injections that affected ovulation.

We tried everything. We were statistically anomalous. Our chances were growing slim; our options were fading.

We passed from the simplest to the most complicated techniques. We stopped having traditional sex and instead I handed over my contribution and she handed over hers and some men in a laboratory tried to make my sperm and her eggs fall in love with one another. Without us.

But not even that was possible.

Out of the fifteen chances, using three different methods, we only had one chance left for success.

For almost five years of our relationship, sex became almost non-existent. For five years, going into a room and handing over my spermatozoa was the norm, as was returning a few hours later to pick up a piece of paper telling me about the speed, quality and quantity of my donation.

It was difficult for me. It was more difficult for her. She put on weight, she was frustrated, she was constantly having fertilized eggs stuck into her. The list of side effects was endless: I can't go through it without feeling trapped again, like I'm sinking, out of my depth.

We carried on doing whatever it was that was asked of us, but towards the end we didn't speak about it. It became taboo.

Even the people who manage to conceive using these methods never talk about it, never talk about their suffering, their *via dolorosa*.

We still felt that we were somehow out of the ordinary, a couple tilting against windmills that only we could see.

I should add that I had always struggled with the idea of having a child. I'd thought that it'd be a dwarf, and the thought pained me because the world simply isn't made for short people.

Everything towers over you, just out of reach.

I guess you must be thinking that all of this is why we broke up. The truth is, it is and it isn't.

Something happened, something that made me remember Mr Martin and George for the first time in years. I had buried them away in the depths of my mind. I'd forgotten them; they were no more than memories from back when I was ten years old, or thirteen, and once I'd grown up the memories left me, they disappeared. When I stopped being a dwarf, I lost them as well. They stayed back there with the smaller version of me, stowed away, forgotten.

But this thing happened. The pearls, the Polaroid photos,

the roulette wheels, the dancing, the dancing with shop mannequin and punch bag: it all came back. It was incredible that time had snatched all this away from me.

And here's what happened. With only one treatment left to go, they said that she was pregnant. It was the happiest moment of our life. We went crazy. We even started to have sex again, proper sex.

But when she was six months pregnant, we lost the baby. They didn't know why, but these things do happen, and there was still one more treatment available to us. The doctor thought that all of this, even though it had been terrible, meant that it was still possible for us to have children. We decided to try one more time, but then he told us something I couldn't deal with. He told us that the child we'd lost had been a dwarf. I didn't expect that. I was shocked. I didn't want a child who was a dwarf.

Suddenly transported back to my own days as a dwarf, I remembered all the diamonds I had met when I had been one. Their lessons and their advice meant that I didn't give up on growing. But my future child might not be as lucky as me, might not ever meet those pearls who would help him, who would allow him to learn to trust himself.

It was all too much for me. So I decided not to go ahead with the last round of treatment. We had one more chance of getting pregnant, but I didn't want to go on, I didn't want the child, and I didn't even know if we'd get the child. Fourteen rounds of treatment down the line, our chances of success were extremely slim.

My refusal was the full stop on our relationship.

Everything fell to pieces after that. We were shipwrecked, a couple breaking apart. I sank into my work, looking for other children.

You know how you sometimes feel that the world is too much for you, and everything around you is off-kilter, moving at a different speed, that you don't feel comfortable around anyone and all you want to do is to stop thinking, even if only for a moment?

Well, I was that lost, lost in a way that you'll only understand if you've been in that state of mind yourself, when everything slips away from you and nothing is important any more.

She left me because I was looking for other children. She left the house and emptied all the drawers. On that day, she gave me an ultimatum. Either I was to start looking for our child, the one she and I would have together, or else she would leave. And I told her that I didn't want to go looking again.

When she left me, I felt I was lost, a dwarf again, that I had to start all over again, from the beginning. With George and Mr Martin. They were the blocks on which I started to build myself again as a person; without them, I would have fallen apart.

And here, in this room, the room that belonged to the other Izan, I felt for the first time the loss of our son. It was almost unbearable to see our dream made reality like this.

'Now, do you think you should read the letter that the kidnapper sent?' the father asked.

I knew that I didn't have a choice. I was once again up against an implacable 'must'. I had to focus my mind on this vanished Izan, the one who had left a distraught family behind. I had to forget my own Izan, the one who made me a stranger to myself, the symbol of all my fears.

20

Be Who You Are or Become the Person You Believe You Are

And so here I am again, in the middle of an empty room, feeling the double weight of my loss.

My own experience as a lost boy led me to look around the room very slowly, very carefully. I sat down on the bed. The father gave me the letter. It was a standard-issue one, typed in twelve-point Arial, not giving any clues, neutral in style. Like so many of the letters I've read.

But this one didn't ask for any ransom. It asked for 'respect', for the father to make a public apology. It asked him to call a press conference and explain that he had made a mistake.

This was new. I kept reading. The author of the letter had been sent to prison for eight years for paedophilia, even though the judge, Izan's father, had known that there was no evidence against him. This was all extremely unusual: the letter was seething with passion and anger.

I looked at the father. 'Does this man exist?'

The father gave me his police file.

'Have you really not called the police?' I asked.

'It says in the letter that if I do, he'll kill my son,' the man replied, not daring to look me in the eye.

I carried on reading and saw that the warning was just as explicit as the boy's father had said.

It also said that the boy would only be released if the official rectification was published; if not, then he would end up becoming what he had been accused of being. And his victim would be Izan.

I had to read this threat twice. Stunned by its cruelty, I re-read it for a third time. I said nothing to the father: it caused him too much pain.

I took the police report, looking for the photograph of the criminal. His face was normal enough. There was also the photograph of the child who had accused him, and his statement.

The boy said that he had been abused at his school, where the criminal worked, carrying out pool maintenance. Eight years had passed since the events.

'Was the boy telling the truth?' I asked the father, looking for his opinion as a lawyer.

He nodded, without going into details.

'How can you be so sure?' I insisted.

'Because the child gave a very detailed report. Because of the look on his face. Because of how scared he was. Because all the circumstantial evidence pointed to the fact that he was right, that he had been abused.'

'And you aren't going to make any public acknowledgement that you made a mistake?'

'No, I can't, out of respect for the other boy.'

'Can I speak with him? Does he still live on Capri?'

'You're going to believe that screwed-up paedophile kid-napper?' the father asked, furious.

'No, but we can at least try doing what he asks in the letter.' I read out the relevant part: '"Speak to Nicholas. Ask him why he lied."'

The father took a while before saying anything. He didn't like the idea at all.

'All right. I'll arrange for you to see him. I'll come with you,' he added.

'I'd prefer to go alone,' I replied.

He didn't insist; he was obviously disconcerted. But I was relieved: I didn't want to have this man, both a judge and a father, present when I spoke to the boy.

'You can take my car and I'll give you directions to his parents' house. Do you know Capri?'

I nodded. I did know it, a little. We left the room. I was going to close the door behind me, but the father stopped me, saying that he wanted his son to find the door open when he came home. Little details like that really touch me. I gave him the letter back.

'Do you realize that we only have two hours to go before we run out of time?' the father asked me, terrified.

'I know, I know.'

I got into the car, put the address into the GPS, felt for the bag with the rings in my pocket, and went off to find the other boy, who I imagined must be feeling pretty lost too.

The father looked out at me from behind the fence that ran around his house. I could see how scared he was, one hundred thousand times more scared than a child about to have his tonsils taken out. I also saw the grandmother, and felt her energy, standing at a distant window.

I had to find and speak to this teenager, the one with all the answers, knowing that if he hadn't lied, then the life of a child was in danger.

I felt scared; I was responsible for so much. Two hours was a very short time to get someone to confess to a lie that they've been keeping for the past eight years. Also, the lie had no doubt been covered up by now with several more.

On the way, I considered ringing my ex-girlfriend and telling her that I had found the child that we had thought was just a simple gust of wind. But I knew I shouldn't.

And I realized that, for the first time in my life, I had not gone through the bedside table of a kidnapped child.

I stopped thinking about myself, and focused on the case again. Moments like these pulse with adrenaline. It was like a game, a game I was playing against the clock. I had to think up my tactics quickly, and they had to work before the hundred and twenty minutes I had left ran out. If they didn't, the unthinkable would happen.

I had an idea. Sometimes a strange approach works better than a straightforward one. I called the missing child's father.

'Have the boy wait for me outside his house. I have to take him somewhere.'

Hopefully this was a good idea. Hopefully.

I put my foot down, knowing that I was staking

everything on a single card. Perhaps this was my game, the one that got my adrenaline going like nothing else could, as Mr Martin had said.

I hoped that I had been dealt a good hand. I accelerated even more.

21

The Son Inside the Son

I picked up Nicholas from in front of another white house. He couldn't have been more than fifteen. He must have been around seven when he was abused.

He looked at me and said nothing. He got into the car as if under duress. Perhaps Izan had felt the same. I felt a little bit like a kidnapper myself.

He sat in the passenger's seat, but still said nothing. I didn't speak to him. He was blond, slim and attractive. He glanced at me out of the corner of his eye.

I drove off towards the place I had in mind. I needed to find somewhere that wouldn't be familiar to him. It needed to be far away from his parents, somewhere just out of his comfort zone. I was sure I knew exactly where to go.

And I knew that he would want to tell me if he had been lying, I felt it in the energy he radiated. But his wish to tell me was one thing, and his instinct another. It's hard to disobey your own body.

We drove in silence. I felt the time slipping by, escaping me. I thought about Izan and hoped that my plan would work.

Finally, we reached the Capri lighthouse. Mr Martin's

favourite – his son. We got out of the car, and the kid followed me at a distance. I approached the tower; the door was open.

I went in and took out the most precious object that I had ever known – the red bag, George's son. I hadn't been wrong: 'My son is inside another son.' I don't know how he had guessed that this lighthouse was Mr Martin's son, but it didn't surprise me in the least that he had.

'This punch bag belonged to a great friend of mine,' I told the boy. 'He taught me that it can do all kinds of things, but, most importantly, it can make you braver and get rid of all your anger. In my lifetime, I've met two really special people. And I think that I met those people – they had to be a part of my life – so that one day you and I would end up standing here. Sometimes the world seems very complicated, like a puzzle that you don't understand until you find the very last piece. Now, listen to me, Nicholas, I need to find the lost boy, I need to find Izan. I've never met him, but I think I created him, a while ago, on a beach, standing next to a woman I lost only recently. And I'll only get her back if I follow the advice of a hundred-year-old woman who just wants to see her grandson again. I'm not going to ask you anything about it. I'm not going to interrogate you, or punish you. All I want you to do is hit this bag as hard as you can.'

The boy said nothing, nothing at all.

I hung the bag from the lighthouse door. Two magical objects set together. All I had to do now was wait for the magic to take effect.

The boy glanced over at me a couple of times. It didn't seem like he was paying me much attention.

But, eventually, he went over to the bag.

I saw him thinking, reaching for his anger, his fear, his problems. And then he hit the bag. Weakly at first, but then with greater and greater force.

I knew that with each blow this child was feeling what I had felt so many years before on the boat. I was sure that he felt the bag absorbing all his anger and leaving him at peace.

Witnessing this moved me deeply. The punch bag, the lighthouse and the Capri sunset. I looked at him as he kept on swinging, each punch accompanied by louder and louder shouts of relief and release.

Time went by, the boy went on fighting, fighting against himself, and I stood by, waiting. I knew that the truth would come out.

And then he broke down.

He cried, he cried so much. He babbled and groaned, leaning against the bag and then standing upright and hitting it again; it was almost as if he were dancing with it.

I saw how deeply entrenched the lie was within him, the many years it had been there. He hadn't enjoyed lying and now all his pain was coming out.

I ended up hugging him. I understood him. Somehow, I felt the same as he did. We were both lost, running away from our own truths.

I didn't need to know any more, I didn't need to know the reasons that had led him to behave in the way he did. I cared for him.

I called the boy's father and told him to send his announcement to the newspapers. I knew that the man who was holding Izan captive would let him go now; he wouldn't cause him any harm. I was sure he would keep his word.

All I had to do now was be brave. I needed to go and speak to my third pearl, my third diamond, my third energy, the third part of me scattered across the world. The hundred-year-old woman who would give birth to my new life.

22

You Tell Me to Come . . . and I Come

The next morning, Izan was asleep in his bed and I was standing with the hundred-year-old woman in a garden, by some trees that were almost as old as her.

And it was there, standing on the lawn beneath the cloudy Capri sky, that she asked me the questions I've already told you about. 'Don't you want your whole life to be happy? To leave behind the things that hurt you? Don't you want to feel that you're in control of your life, and not just drifting along in its rip tide? Do you want to control your life? Do you want to be in charge of every moment? Do you?'

And I said yes, enthusiastically, hoping that this would mark the path into my new world.

I had got off that old bicycle of a life I had spent so many years pedalling. All I had to show for it were two pearls, a job that dominated every waking moment, and a relationship that had broken down because I didn't want to be the father of a dwarf.

This old woman, so beautiful to me, couldn't possibly realize how much I had been in need of her advice.

At that point in my life, without anyone who cared enough to tell me, I only had sufficient energy to last me maybe two more years or so. At that rate I would never get to be as old as George, or Mr Martin.

It was yet another reason to stand in awe of them. I think that you should be in awe of anyone who reaches the age of sixty. You've got to be brave to live through so many years.

I've always wondered why, if it's so easy to leave the game, why we carry on playing it?

I thought the old woman must have been reading my thoughts; at least that's what her eyes, studying me so closely, seemed to suggest.

I could sense she was very wise. And best of all, she wanted to share her wisdom with me.

'What I am about to tell you,' she said in a very low voice, so low that I had to get very close to her, 'what I am about to tell you will only be of use to you if you take it as the focus, the guiding star of your life. If you mix and muddle it with other philosophies or principles, then it'll never take you anywhere.'

I nodded obediently.

'It's made up of two ideas.' She had raised her voice now, but I didn't move away from her. 'First, you must remember that loving someone is always worth more than being loved. Loving can move worlds, can make them stand still. But being loved when you aren't loving in return will just make you lazy and slow.'

She paused as dawn broke over Capri. I couldn't even begin to take it all in. I had let myself be loved my whole life. Maybe that wasn't enough.

'The second most valuable thing to know as you move forward is that we have all spent all of our lives, ever since we were children, asking ourselves the question "What do I like?" What do I like to eat, what do I like to wear, what do I like to play with, what do I like to study, what work do I like to do, who do I like to have as my friends, who do I like to be in love with, how do I like to have sex. And it is this "What do I like?" that defines our world. It gives us the impression that, if we like something, then that's the thing we must pursue, the path we must follow, the desire that truly moves us. But that's simply not the case. What we like doesn't show us the path we need to follow; neither does what we don't like. Sometimes, we just need to follow the path of indifference, and do those things that neither appeal to, nor appal us. You should understand this. You have to trust in yourself, not in the things that you think you like. Your path is not marked out by the things that you like, but by the markers you yourself set down.'

After saying this, she hugged me and began walking back towards the house, humming to herself: 'If you tell me to come, I'll drop everything. But tell me to come.' She stopped halfway and lit a cigarette. And I swear that, in that moment, she was the living image of the casino employee Mr Martin had loved. She looked the same from far away and from close up. Perhaps it was her.

I knew that those two pieces of advice would shape the next few years of my life, even if I was in no hurry to put them into practice at that precise moment. Because, before doing anything else, I just wanted to see the cloudy dawn rise over Capri, and then set out on my own path through the world.

I could see Izan looking out at me from the window of the house. I turned to look at him and waved. He waved back.

I knew at that moment that I needed to have my own Izan. To love. I would love him so much, more than I had ever been loved myself.

And I didn't care at all what he was like, how tall he was, whatever I thought when I looked at him. I didn't care what I liked or did not like. I didn't care what people thought.

I took out my phone and wrote her a message: 'I want to have Izan. I can't live without him, without you.'

I waited for the reply to come back.

It took a couple of minutes. The sun had just risen fully when the message tone went off. It was the soundtrack to the dawn.

She had replied: 'Yes, you can.'

I smiled. We were back to our codes again, caught up in our *Breathless* getaway.

Maybe this could be the ultimate getaway – maybe my escape hadn't, as I'd thought, all come to an end back when I left Capri so many years ago.

I smiled and wrote the reply she was waiting for. 'I can live without you, but I don't want to. Why not come to Capri? You have to meet Izan, the boy we made out of a gust of wind, and you have to see the lighthouse: it was this man's favourite, this man who also loved women who spun roulette wheels and who lost his heart to a shop mannequin; and you have to see the underground chamber where I developed diamonds and pearls, where there are bags filled with remnants of lives, and you have to meet this hundred-year-old woman who thinks that the lyrics of that old song should be, "If you tell me to come, I'll drop everything . . . but tell me to come".'

This time, the reply came almost as soon as I'd sent the message. I felt a breeze from Menorca dance over my face, like a sigh, just as the screen lit up.

'You tell me to come . . . and I come.'

And my life started to turn, to move forward once again. Slowly, I did two things I had wanted to do for some time. I put my father's ring on my finger. And then I took the silver lighthouse, put the monocle over my left eye and watched the clouds moving away as the sun came out. And the half-hidden engraving, the 'Mi' that was now wrapped around my index finger, shone out and shone brightly.

I had become myself. The world began to turn again.